ENDORSEMENTS/REVIEW

'In the book *The Ladder to Aca*... insightful analysis of the causes of deteriorating q... cation in Nigeria and offers thoughtful, pragmati... can excel within the constraints imposed by the ...ent. The author proposes a conceptual framewor... ; to the declining quality of education—**FIDEAS** ..., Determination, Effort, Achievement, and Success). She subsequently used this framework effectively in organizing the book.

'The ideas presented in the book are clear and represent an original voice. Particularly striking is Chinwe Okoli's proven ability to articulate central issues in a debate and to communicate them persuasively and effectively to a targeted audience, which, in this case, is the Nigeria youth, including current, aspiring, and future students. This book is timely. It fills an important void that, unaddressed, will impede Nigerian's ability to be competitive in an increasingly global society. The ideas in this book represent one original solution, among many, to mitigating the rapidly declining quality of secondary and post-secondary education in Nigeria. I admire and commend Chinwe Okoli for her vision, thoughtfulness, hard work, and persistence in undertaking this endeavour, especially for someone who has just graduated from the University of Nigeria, Nsukka, and is currently performing her National Youth Service Corps (NYSC) in Abuja, Nigeria.'

—*Professor Forster Ndubisi, PhD, FCELA, FASLA*
Head of Department, Landscape Architecture and Urban Planning,
A and M University, College Station, Texas, USA (2013)

Timely and Timeless Work

'Like all remarkable works, Chinwe Okoli's *Ladder to Academic Excellence* is both a timely and timeless work. It comes at a time when education in Nigeria is generally believed to have failed both the students and the nation and therefore needs a radical overhaul. And in the long term, the book provides an enduring guide for a future of academic excellence. Although the subtitle is "A Hands-on Guide for Students", I suggest that both the government and the education sector will do well to pay serious attention to this book. For it is when the right education is provided in the correct environment that the student stands the best chance of achieving excellence. In this sense, the author has provided an invaluable guide for the nation as a whole.'

—*Dr Eddie Iroh, OON*
Author and Former Director General of Radio Nigeria
London, United Kingdom (2013)

'Chinwe Okoli, in this book, has most powerfully in a highly scholarly manner perfectly articulated the fact that academic death is committing an intellectual suicide and that every student can be better than he is, if such a person works harder, utilizing every good opportunity and means in climbing the academic ladder through what she called **FIDEAS** (Focus, Ideas, Determination, Efforts, Achievements, and Success). Following the author's FIDEAS strictly with every measure postulated, academic indolence and school jamborees will be a thing of the past, paving way for brighter future, limitless opportunities in the world, rightful and proper positioning in the global struggle to live a meaningful life. *The Ladder to Academic Excellence* is a book to be read, chewed, and digested. Therefore, I highly recommend it to everybody especially the students of both secondary and tertiary institutions—universities, polytechnics, colleges of education. I also recommend it to education policymakers of every nation, to educational instructors, and to all parents.'

—*Rev Fr Vincent O. Nnabude*
Catholic Diocese of Nnewi and the Author The Banquet of the Virgins

'*The Ladder to Academic Excellence* is a combination of innovative insights, school lessons, and real-life experiences which give students a fresh direction in attaining higher heights in their academic pursuit in preparation for future roles of nation-building. This book is a great effort and well packaged with great ideas and tons of practical advice. Read, enjoy, and excel.

—*Kayode Olagunju, PhD*
Assistant Corps Marshal
Federal Road Safety Corps, Nigeria

'At a time when the youths of other lands are aiming for the stars and ours are groping in the dark, we need pinprick such as this to awaken us, students and their parents, to awaken us to consequences of our present choices. This book is an audacious attempt to waken us from our slumber. I recommend it to all who care for our society tomorrow.'

—*Rev Fr (Dr) H. E. Ichoku*
Director of Academic Planning Unit, University of Nigeria, Nsukka

'The deterioration in our education sector ranks among the most critical and disturbing in our current litany of national woes and challenges. The author's work been a package of solution in its merit, therefore is a step in the right direction because it is a good example of the kind of practical response we need in our present circumstances. It is an attempt for an answer or a solution!

'I commend not just the work which is relatively far-reaching in both content and quality, but also the spirit behind it—the spirit of action for solution, the spirit of sacrifice and giving! I strongly recommend the book not only to students, but also to all who have the responsibility to provide academic guide, including parents, guardians, and teachers. It is a useful workbook for them.

'Beyond the book's emphasis on education and student, the work equally has some flavour of general inspiration. In fact, "A Ladder to Success Using the Student as Example" can pass for another fitting title for the book. Any reader can replace the "student" with himself/herself. In almost all spheres of human endeavour, achievement or success to a large extent depends on Focus, Ideas, Determination and Effort (FIDEAS), which is highlighted extensively by the author. The same way and in the same measure these keywords are useful and relevant to the student, they are equally useful and relevant to whoever is aspiring to achieve or succeed. Therefore, the book in my view is a good read for all.'

—*Uchenna Anigbata*
Lagos

'The book is remarkable in that it is very well researched, with illustrations and quotations. It shows the passion of the author to have young students excel in their studies in spite of the challenges in the society, rather than give excuses for failure and substandard work.

The discipline to make FIDEAS work reinforces personal integrity, as such, an excellent student will not engage in examination malpractices and other vices. A student who excels through FIDEAS will abhor corruption and be a lighthouse for others in building a nation founded on integrity. I therefore have no hesitation in recommending this book to all students and youths as a guide to achieving excellence in their academics and in every life endeavour'.

—*Ekpo Nta, Esq*
Chairman,
Independent Corrupt Practices and other Related Offences Commission (ICPC)

A

328.41/Mitchell

Parkside Federation Academies
This book is due for return on the date below.

Please look after this book

. 19678 19678

CHINWE OKOLI

Copyright © 2014 by Chinwe Okoli.
chinwejane.okoli@yahoo.com

ISBN:	Softcover	978-1-4990-8662-1
	eBook	978-1-4990-8663-8

All rights reserved. No part of this book may be reproduced or transmitted in any form or by any means, electronic or mechanical, including photocopying, recording, or by any information storage and retrieval system, without permission in writing from the copyright owner.

Images created by Dumeme Ndubisi. Dumemearts.
Twitter: @dumemearts. E mail: dumemearts@gmail.com

This book was printed in the United States of America.

Rev. date: 08/04/2014

To order additional copies of this book, contact:
Xlibris LLC
0-800-056-3182
www.xlibrispublishing.co.uk
Orders@xlibrispublishing.co.uk

Contents

Foreword I 11
Foreword II 13
Preface.. 17
Acknowledgements.. 19
Introduction... 23

Chapter 1.   Falling Standard of Education 29
Chapter 2.   Be Focused 35
Chapter 3.   How Did Your Academic Journey Start? 41
Chapter 4.   Background Never an Obstacle................................... 46
Chapter 5.   Do You Have a Destination?.. 50
Chapter 6.   Fresh in School 57
Chapter 7.   Failure as a Result of Obstacles 60
Chapter 8.   Relationship-Related Obstacles................................... 63
Chapter 9.   Environment-Induced Obstacles 71
Chapter 10. 'You' As Your Own Obstacle....................................... 78
Chapter 11. Other Individual-Related Obstacles........................... 83
Chapter 12. Other External Factors, Problems, Obstacles
             and Their General Effects 95
Chapter 13. How Determined Are You?... 105
Chapter 14. Motivation for Determination 108
Chapter 15. Eliminate Fear and Limiting Belief............................. 115
Chapter 16. You Must Have Attitude 120
Chapter 17. Study Attitude 127
Chapter 18. Other Important Factors and Areas of Interest to Note....... 134
Chapter 19. Achieving Academic Excellence 141
Chapter 20. Take That Decision; You Can Do It 145
Chapter 21. Success and Smiles at Last.. 148
Chapter 22. Keep the Flag Flying High: Personal Development............ 151
Chapter 23. Conclusion... 161

References 165
Endnotes 169

To my Grandmum, Mum, Uncle Uche

Rev Fr Vincent O. Nnabude

and

all who have predilection for excellence.

Foreword I

I am happy and proud to write this short foreword on a piece of work I believe has the potential to dramatically change the lives of millions of our youths. When the author Chinwe Okoli (a 2011 graduate from my alma mater, Department of Economics, University of Nigeria, Nsukka) approached me to write the foreword, I must confess that I was at first sceptical and reluctant. In an age of declining academic standards, I was not sure what quality to expect from a fresh female graduate. As I casually perused through the pages of the manuscript, I could not stop reading. I am pleasantly surprised and proud that our young graduate has written a prodigious book to educate and motivate others to succeed in life.

The Ladder to Academic Excellence is not just a book for academic excellence; it is a book on 'how to succeed in life'. There are several 'how to succeed' books on the shelves, but Chinwe Okoli's is different. It is a blend of research and experience. Several of her illustrations come from her personal experiences as a female student who struggled through the morass and maze of the sometimes-confounding university life to find a bearing in life. I am familiar with several of the principles of success ably presented in the book. In my mentoring sessions with the younger ones, I emphasise three keywords as ingredients of success: focus, hard work, and prayer! This book adumbrates these principles and more.

It is generally acknowledged that Nigeria's educational system has deteriorated over the years, and a majority of its graduates are unemployable. Millions of unemployed and unemployable youths therefore roam our streets, with dire consequences for the present and future economic prospects. Government has a huge role to play to get Nigeria out of the mess. However, there is also a big role for individual responsibility. I have always believed that the best university in the world cannot teach you more than 40 per cent of what you need to know in any subject: you have to figure out the remaining 60 per cent! Here is where personal responsibility, personal effort, focus, discipline, and drive come in, and happily these constitute the focus of this book. This book is therefore about dealing with the remaining 60 per cent, which is critical to achieving the overall success both at the individual and systemic levels.

I strongly commend and recommend this book to all students and young people eager to succeed in life. It is a cookbook for success that everyone would find useful. I also strongly recommend that government educational authorities at all levels in Nigeria as well as ministries in charge of youth development at the state and federal levels should promote the massive circulation of this book to our youths.

—Professor Chukwuma Charles Soludo, CFR
January 2013

Foreword II

Education is generally understood as 'a form of learning in which knowledge, skills, and habits of a group of people are transferred from one generation to the next through teaching, training, research, or simply through autodidacticism. Generally, it occurs through any experience that has a formative effect on the way one thinks, feels, or acts'. This concept of education from Wikipedia provides a view of one of the most important human realities that ensures the preservation, development, and transmission of all that is worthwhile in humanity. Human beings as conscious and rational beings instinctively and consciously embrace education as a veritable tool for self and societal improvement and development, a vehicle for the preservation and transmission of culture and instrument for development. No wonder all responsible persons, societies, governments, and religious bodies place a high premium on education.

Education has occupied a very central place in Nigeria with the government at all levels taking interest in it. The various Christian missions in Nigeria were prime movers of education with the government giving support and regulations. Under this regime, education advanced and achieved its goal of producing disciplined, literate, socially well-adjusted, and God-fearing persons. Unfortunately, when the various governments in the federation embarked on government monopoly of education, education expanded, but the standards went down. Even though the country witnessed 'government complete and dynamic intervention and active participation in education' (as claimed in a report), the politicisation and endemic systemic corruption in Nigeria introduced the viruses that have crippled education in Nigeria and produced waves of educational refugees to Europe, America, Asia, and other African countries, especially Ghana.

What are the viruses? The most virulent of them is *achievement without commensurate effort*. People expect results that are not matched by input. The corruption in the Nigerian society whereby people without visible means of livelihood flaunt ill-gotten wealth, especially wealth acquired through exploitation of public resources, killed the effort. In education, it introduced examination malpractices in their various forms and shapes. It killed the resolve of both teachers and learners to follow the narrow way to success through discipline and hard work. Teachers see themselves as civil servants who are neither civil nor interested in service. They are primarily interested in conditions of service which they fight for with all the tools at their disposal including abandoning the people they are employed to teach. They are not averse to abusing their position to make money and take undue advantage of their student by selling handouts and grades, leaking question papers and asking for sexual favours. When teachers become cheaters, what would you expect from their students?

The students on their part would not see the rationale for attending classes and 'wasting' their time studying when they can get the result by paying either with money or in kind. No wonder the standard of education went down so drastically in public schools and universities that many 'educated' people in Nigeria are not just half-baked, but in fact illiterate. These ignorant and illiterate people are offloaded into the system. And should any serious-minded person be surprised at the inefficiency and lack of productivity in the public services of this country? We are reaping the fruits of the calculated attempts to sacrifice merit and efforts on the altar of 'quota system', connections, influence, state of origin, son/daughter of the soil, and other despicable factors that breed favouritism, mediocrity, inefficiency, and under-productivity. The motivation for achievement of success through discipline and hard work has to be injected back into the system for meaningful development and improvement in our education and in the socio-economic development in general.

This is precisely what Miss Chinwe Okoli is attempting to do. With her personal knowledge, experience, and determination to make a difference, she is talking directly to the young to achieve a turnaround in their lives, to undo the decades of malformation or indeed non-formation to which the society has condemned our young people. She has studied the system and found it wanting in providing the necessary motivation for the young to succeed through due process. She addresses the young in the context of a society that is in deficit of moral values and decency. Indeed, as St Paul wrote, the age is evil but we must redeem it (see Ephesians 5:16). Chinwe is determined to touch the minds and hearts of young people to positively change their attitudes by giving them the reason to do things differently from the way Nigerian system since the end of the civil war is accustomed to doing things. She wants to inculcate and instil mental discipline and moral courage to be different in a positive way.

The book *The Ladder to Academic Excellence* is not only for the school system. It is also for the generality of Nigerians who want a better-organized, more efficient, and more productive society made of men and women of honour and integrity, men and women who are proud of their achievements because they can publicly defend the process of arriving at the results, which are indeed their own. She wants Nigerians not to revel in results but to look closely at the process of getting those results. It is not a secret that as many Nigerians acquire wealth without lawful and morally proven means, so students get results that have no bearing with their actual performance. Chinwe says a capital NO to such scam and counsels all to go through the narrow and difficult path to success, to defendable achievement and success.

Her work is revolutionary. It is going against the current of laxity, following the crowd and seeking the path of least resistance. Looking at all sectors of life, she is going against the popular and 'hot' lifestyle to preach a lifestyle patterned on verifiable process of vision, planning, determination, and worthwhile achievement which she stylistically called **FIDEAS**, meaning **F**ocus, **I**deas, **D**etermination, **E**fforts, **A**chievement, and **S**uccess. Going through these six important and indispensable steps on the ladder of excellence both in academic pursuit and in other worthwhile pursuits in life, one will see the **REVOLUTION** set in motion by Chinwe. Indeed I am looking to what St Paul wrote to the Romans: '*Do not model your behaviour on the contemporary world, but let the renewing of your minds transform you, so that you may discern for yourselves what is the will of God—what is good and acceptable and mature*' (Romans 12:2). **FIDEAS** is a *transformation agenda* which everybody who loves himself or herself and who loves our country should embrace for self-improvement and for societal transformation. **FIDEAS** is indeed a bundle of *fine ideas*!

I am confidently presenting this book to governments, churches, and the society in general in this country and beyond to adopt for the pedagogy of the young so that we may train up a new crop of young men and women who are properly focused and adequately motivated to change the face of Nigeria. It can be done with public support. Indeed, some governments in

FOREWORD II

this country are really worried about the outcome of our educational system and want to do something about the rot in the educational system. The book *The Ladder to Academic Excellence* is a powerful tool if adopted and used to initiate a revolution in our educational system as a means of setting fire to the society that is corrupt and inefficient for a brand-new society to emerge. Nobody should wait on government to initiate this revolution. Parents can start; children can embrace it, and any group can key into it by studying and applying the rich insights and methodology of *The Ladder to Academic Excellence*. Let us individually and collectively do something to change the system of achievement without commensurate efforts. We can and must change it for us to forge ahead to be respected and proudly so.

By the sweat of your face will you earn your food until you return to the ground as you were taken from it (see Genesis 3:19) is the price humanity will continue to pay since the Fall when human beings listened to the deceptive Satan that convinced Eve that one can go against the Law of God with impunity by reaping where one did not sow. Effort guided by vision and determination is the only way to sustainable and honourable success.

—Most Rev Hilary Paul Odili Okeke
Bishop of the Catholic Diocese of Nnewi

UNIVERSITY OF NIGERIA
OFFICE OF THE VICE-CHANCELLOR

Vice-Chancellor: Professor Bartho N. Okolo, Ph. D. (Strathclyde)　　　　Phone: (+234) - 706 706 1314, 705 977 8444, 708 861 7000

Preface

The book will serve as a useful source of support and guidance to students and all those involved in education and mentoring. Drawing mostly from her experience, which is relatively fresh and recent, the author has written in a language that students will understand. She deserves commendation for the foresight, courage and determination that led her to embark on a book project at this stage in her career.

Professor Bartho N. Okolo
Vice-Chancellor

Correspondence: University of Nigeria, Nsukka, Nigeria. Email: vc.unn@unn.edu.ng

Acknowledgements

My overwhelming and foremost gratitude goes to the Most High God, the omnipotent, omniscience, and excellence himself, for granting me the vision and insight through which this book was articulated.

My sincere and undiluted gratitude goes to Most Rev Dr Hillary Odili Okeke, the Catholic bishop of Nnewi diocese, for his fatherly support and encouragement always, for painstakingly reading through the manuscript and writing the endorsement despite his very tight schedule. God bless you always, Daddy.

My ever deep and unalloyed gratitude goes to Rev Fr Vincent Nnabude. I cannot talk about academic excellence without a strong allusion to him. In the same vein, I appreciate Rev Frs Vitalis Anehobi, Linus Iloegesi, Anthony Obele and Cletus Chukwuemeka. May God bless you all forever and continue to guide you in your ministerial duties.

A very special and immense appreciation goes to Mr Chiedu Ndubisi, who, out of his proclivity for excellence, scrupulously and repeatedly edited the manuscript. May God reward him abundantly.

My unfathomable gratitude goes to an erudite and amiable scholar, Prof C. C. Soludo, for accepting to read the manuscript and write the foreword notwithstanding his numerous engagements. His predilection for excellence serves as example and strong motivation for the students. God bless him immensely.

My very deep and sincere appreciation to Mr Obi Ezeude, The President of Beloxxi Group, for his financial support and encouragement at the very critical stage of this work. In the same vein, my sincere appreciation goes to Mr Peter Obi, the immediate past governor of Anambra State for his support and encouragement. God bless you always.

ACKNOWLEDGEMENTS

My overwhelming thanks also goes to Dr Oby Ezekwesili, who, despite her very tight schedule, found time to peruse my manuscript and was also present at the commissioning of this project. May the everlasting arms of God continue to uphold you.

My profound gratitude goes to Samuel Udeh through whose very unusual call at 3:45 a.m. on that blessed day woke me up to the thought of writing this book. God really used you as a messenger. May God bless you immensely.

My loyalty and sincere appreciation goes to the National Youth Service Corps (NYSC) scheme for giving me the platform to execute this project. My very deep appreciation goes to Brigadier General N. T. OKore-Affiah (DG NYSC in my service year 2012/2013) for his support, also Mr Frank Ekpunobi, Mrs Arokoyo, Mrs Linda Amugo, Mrs Erege, Mrs Iwolo, and all NYSC officials that facilitated this project. May God reward you all.

My unalloyed gratitude goes to Prof Batho Okolo (the vice chancellor of the University of Nigeria) for being there for his students. I appreciate your sincere contribution, sir. God bless you abundantly. In the same vein, I heartily appreciate the staff and students of the University of Nigeria, Nsukka (my alma mater), and those of Government Secondary School Jikwoyi, Abuja, where I did the NYSC programme. My association and interaction with you all formed my basic experience upon which this book was written. I appreciate every minute spent with you all. God bless you all.

A very special appreciation goes to all who reviewed and commented on the manuscript: Prof Forster Ndubisi, Dr Eddie Iroh, Prof C. C. Aguh, Rev Fr Dr H. E. Ichoku, Dr Kayode Olagunju, Dr Abraham Nwankwo (DG DMO Nigeria), Dr Alex Ekwueme (Ide Oko), Mr Ekp Nta, Esq, Engr Odili Ojukwu, Engr Martin Ibe, Barr Emenike Mgbemena, Dr Chima Nwanguma, Dr W. M. Fonta, and Dr Mich Akabogu. I really appreciate your efforts, constructive criticisms, and time. God bless you all.

My sincere appreciation also goes to Duememe Ndubisi (@Dumemearts) for creating the pictorial designs and also to Lisa, Kay, Rachel, Jean and all members of the Xlibris Publishing family, it's my pleasure working with you all.

My most profound gratitude goes to my ever-caring uncle, Uche Anigbata, for his unquantifiable support and encouragement throughout the course of this work. You are wonderfully amazing. May the joy of the Lord never depart from your family.

My hearty and sincere gratitude goes to my beloved Mum, Mrs Amaka Ononeze (Ebeano special). Her encouragement, advice, sincere love, and moral support made me who I am today; she is the best mum in the whole world. In the same vein, I appreciate my beloved grandmum, Mrs Elizabeth Okoli (Idigo). I love you, Mama.

I heartily appreciate my beloved uncle Mr Christopher Okoli and his lovely queen Mrs Onyinye Okoli, Augustine Okoli (half a million; young shall grow aluminium), Mr Uzochukwu Okoli. My sweet kid siblings, Ebere, Anuli, Uche, and Ekene. My little cousins, Daniel, Ngozi, Chigozie, Anuli, Somtoo, Anointing, Onyedika, and Chiamaka. You all are wonderful and I love you all.

My profound gratitude to my special friends Ijeoma Ezeagu Agada, Ugochinyere Onyeka, Idakwoji Adejoh, Chris Okoli, Anthony Okafor(First class Statistician), Ikenna Okoye, Chidi Achikasim, Peter and Paul Hiikyaa (PIP classic records), Augustine Aguh, Ekene Aguegbo (first-class economist), Chiamaka Ezigbo (first-class engineer), Chiamaka Igboanusi, Reginald Ogbuji, Ken Ugwoke, and Ugoo Aghaji, for their support and sincere encouragement in difficult times. You guys are wonderful.

Introduction

Education is a companion which no misfortune can depress, no crime can destroy, no enemy can alienate, no disposition can enslave, at home a friend, abroad an introduction, in solitude a solace and in society an ornament. It gives at once grace and government to genius. Without it what is man? A splendid slave, a seasoning savage.[1]

—Joseph Addison (1672-1719), English essayist,
poet, playwright, and politician

Education should be the priority of every nation that wants to remain relevant in the comity of nations. It is for its great import that Victor Hugo, a nineteenth-century French poet, dramatist, and novelist, said, *'He who opens a school door, closes a prison'*[2], and Joseph Addison remarked that *'what sculpture is to a block of marble, education is to a human soul'*.[3]

It is not only beneficial to an individual, but also to the nation and the world at large. In the words of Nelson Mandela, a former South African president and a 1993 Nobel Prize laureate, *'Education is the most powerful weapon, which you can use to change the world'*.[4] Barack Obama, the president of the United States, in an address to the Joint Session of Congress on 24 February 2009, said, *'In a global economy, where the most valuable skill you can sell is your knowledge, a good education is no longer just a pathway to opportunity—it is a pre-requisite'*.[5] He also said in his press conference on 17 March 2009 that *'the countries who out-educate us today will out-compete us tomorrow'*.[6] These statements largely demonstrate the role education plays in the freedom and advancement of man.

It is for this reason that the rate of academic failure or the falling standards of education in nations, including Nigeria and sub-Saharan African countries, becomes a matter of grave concern to parents, governments, and indeed all stakeholders in education. The implied waste of enormous resources invested in education in these times of dwindling government resources amidst competing needs can hardly be afforded or justified. Like a crack in a foundation or a structural defect in an engineering master plan, academic failure, if unchecked, will gradually culminate into a material deficiency in the general resource quality of a nation. It therefore poses very grave danger to the overall socio-economic, political, and technological development of a nation.

In Nigeria, for instance, the result of the West African Senior Secondary Certificate Examination (WASSCE), the ordinary level examinations in West Africa over the years, shows that less than a quarter of the registered candidates each year pass with a minimum of five credits, including English language and mathematics. The same level of performance is also experienced at the ordinary level results of the National Examination Council (NECO) and Joint Admission and Matriculation Board (JAMB), which are entrance examinations to higher institutions in Nigeria. These results show progressive decline each year despite the attendant high level of examination malpractice in the system, which the other stakeholders appear to be working hard to control. Consequently, the present-day product of the country's education system is barely literate. A good number cannot make a correct sentence in English, cannot convey a simple message, or articulate a simple idea. Others who could have performed better lacked the necessary academic foundation and guidance to do so.

As an undergraduate, I have had cause to admonish my fellow students who approached their academic work with apathy. Even with minimal guidance and mentoring, they improved tremendously and afterwards realized their full academic dreams. I discovered that a lot of students under-achieve, not for reasons of low intellectual endowment or being naturally dull, but for lack of focus and determination. They are easily distracted by peer group pressures, lack personal and academic discipline and simple guide on what they need to do to properly harness their academic potentials. As it is not physically possible to reach every student personally, I thought I could add value to the lives of these groups of students by conveying my ideas through a book. By so doing, I would be achieving my dream of reaching out to as many students as possible on a turnaround strategy that will reposition them towards attaining their academic goals and becoming very useful members of the society. That will also be my little contribution towards raising the ebbing academic standard. It is my desire to revive the dying, dwindling, deteriorating, or dormant scholastic spirit in many students, especially in Nigeria and Africa and other parts of the world experiencing similar untoward educational development. It is this desire that gave birth to this book.

In this work, I drew a lot from my personal experience as a student and a teacher, from opinions and experiences of scholars, leaders, thinkers, and philosophers, from interaction with students, from observations and experiments, as well as from academic research on youths and academic work.

This book has been organized in six parts, which is referred to as **FIDEAS**, an acronym for **F** = focus, **I** = Ideas, **D** = determination, **E** = Efforts, **A** = Achievement, and **S**=Success, aptly depicted below:

The first section emphasizes the importance of remaining *focused in the reason for being in school*. It is only when this reason is properly articulated and defined that one stands the chance of ever succeeding. The importance of having a goal that a student will focus on throughout his/her stay in school is stressed in this section. The actions and inactions that could impede the attainment of one's goal are discussed in the next section that is referred to as 'Ideas'. Then the student, having a reasonable knowledge of these obstacles in the third section, reaches a decision to be *determined* to attain the set goal. The fourth section explores those necessary next steps and *efforts* needed for the students to surmount the identified challenges and *achieve* their academic goals. The last section discusses the numerous opportunities that await a successful and excellent achiever at the top of the ladder to academic excellence—*the fruits of success*.

A focus on the student and his/her academic challenges is maintained throughout this book, considering that the student is the major stakeholder in the academic system. In this respect, 'Efforts' have been made to put together simple but very effective and hands-on tips and strategies as part of the solution to the deterioration in the education sector, which is not only a national embarrassment, but also a major threat to the socio-political stability and future competitiveness of a nation.

The book may also be of interest to government, policymakers, teachers, parents, and other stakeholders as they escalate efforts at addressing other challenges and factors responsible for the deteriorating state of education in the country. They may find this book useful as part of their policy inventory in their quest to rejuvenate the Nigerian educational system.

The book, if used properly, can serve as a sound guide for any student willing to be distinguished from the *Joneses*. It could help in identifying and dealing with the weaknesses as well as provide a guide on how to discover and deploy potentials in a student. It could serve as a companion to any student who wants to be outstanding, a source of inspiration, motivation, and point of reference to others in the academic world. Arnold Schwarzenegger, an actor and politician (the thirty-eighth governor of California), said, '*Just remember you can't climb the ladder of Success with your hands in your pockets.*'[7] And the only place where success comes before work is in the dictionary.

SECTION ONE

Focus

CHAPTER ONE

Falling Standard of Education

My great concern is not whether you have failed, but whether you are content with your failure.[8]

—Abraham Lincoln

At independence in 1960, Nigeria had high hopes to transform its sleepy colonial society into a modern society, inspired from within. As would be expected, only a small proportion of all professional service posts were held by Nigerians. Most of the trade and industry was foreign-owned,— managed, and—controlled. Consequently, the urgent challenge of education and thrust of educational policy at that time was to produce high-level professionals to replace the expatriates in the administration of the country and to train skilled manpower to be in charge of the emerging industrial sector, where activity was picking up as a result of the 'import substitution' development strategy being pursued by the newly independent state.

It is noteworthy that the products of first six Nigerian universities, namely, Universities of Ibadan, Ile Ife, Lagos, Benin, Zaria, and the University of Nigeria, Nsukka, competed favourably with the products of even the Ivy League university in the United States of America and the universities of Cambridge, Oxford, and London for admission into their post-graduate courses.[9] These students, often with record-breaking performances, also competed for employment in Fortune 500 companies alongside their counterparts from other parts of the world. By the 1980s, the country had one of the best higher education systems in the developing world, offering instruction at an international standard in diverse disciplines, and such universities as Ibadan and Ahmadu Bello received global accolades for research in tropical health and agriculture.[10]

The more universities Nigeria establishes, the lower her ranking on the global scale of high-quality higher education. According to the Times Higher Education World University Rankings 2012-2013, no Nigerian university is among the top 6,000 universities of the world. Indeed, only the Universities of Cape Town, Witwatersrand, Stellenbosch, and KwaZulu-Natal, all in South Africa, made the list from the African continent.[11] Even among the contending universities in Africa, the best Nigerian university was ranked number 25, trailing behind some universities in Egypt, South Africa, Tanzania, Kenya, Morocco Burkina Faso, Uganda, Botwana, Ghana and Mozambique. However, in 2014, eleven Nigerian Universities as against four in 2011—Obafemi Awolowo University (25th), University of Lagos (39th), University of Ilorin (57th), Federal University of Technology, Minna (64th), University of Ibadan (70th) University of Nigeria (75th), Amadu Bello University(80th), University of Benin(84th), University of Agriculture, Abeokuta(85th), Covenant University(94th), Madonna University(97th)—made the first 100 universities in Africa.[12] The fact that no Nigerian university feature among the best 6,000[13] in the world and are ranked from position 25 downwards in Africa is symptomatic of a very fundamentally flawed education system.

This same level of decline is also evident in the quality of research. The number of scientific publications from Nigerian universities in 1995 was 711. At the height of its academic excellence in 1981, the output of scientific publications by the Nigerian university system was 1,062. In comparison, South Africa had 3,413; Brazil had 5,440; while India had 14,883; at the time Nigeria could boast of only 711.[14] These three are countries whose scale Nigeria ought to share.

Today, an unusually large fraction of Nigerian graduates are uncompetitive, unemployable, or remain unemployed several years after graduation. There was a case of a master's degree student who could not even spell her name correctly in two successive examinations![15] One begins to wonder how that student got to the master's degree level. There are many of such students and graduates in Nigeria.[16] Consequently, there is now the necessity for substantial retraining of even the best graduates by employers before they can become productve.[17]

Another pointer to the falling standards of education in the country is the decline in academic performance over time at all levels. The results of different examinations at the secondary and tertiary levels in the past decade show a continuous decline in both standards and attitudes. From 1999 to 2010, far less than one-third of the registered candidates who sat for the West African Senior Secondary Certificate examination passed with credits in five subjects, including English and mathematics. The 1999 to 2000 were the worst ever, with less than 8% of the students passing with credits in five subjects. While improvements were recorded between 2001 and 2005, with about 18% of the students passing with five credits, this fell again to about 8% between 2006 and 2008 as shown in the table at the right hand side. This same pattern of performance is repeated in NECO, JAMB, and similar examinations. The situation is actually getting even worse, judging by the 2012 JAMB results where only 3 candidates scored above 300 in contrast to over 2000 candidates the in year 2011. The very poor JAMB result in 2013 led the Honourable Minister of Education to lowering the university entrance benchmark from 200 points to 180[18] points on a 400 grade scale. The same trend was recorded in the recently concluded 2014 JAMB[19] paper and pencil test (PPT) where out of 1,629,102[20] less than 100 candidates scored 250 and above. This is not peculiar to Nigeria but many other developing countries experience similar trend in their educational system.

Table 1: **Summary of candidates with 5 credits in WAEC May/June exams (1999-2008)**

Year	Total entry	5 credits	% with five credits
1999	814596	43099	5.29
2000	725274	57103	7.87
2001	1099296	178054	16.19
2002	1224381	188494	15.35
2003	1039028	200148	19.26
2004	1051246	191938	18.25
2005	1091763	203991	18.68
2006	1184223	110417	9.32
2007	1275832	98133	7.69
2008	1369171	127147	9.29
2009	1250437	321066	25.67
2010	1244801	280310	22.52

SOURCES:
- 1. FME: Nigeria: The Statistics of Education in Nigeria (1999-2005)
- 2. NBS: Social Statistics of Nigeria 2009
- 3. FME: NIGERIA: Digest of Education Statistics (2006-2010)

*Including English and Mathematics

The most disturbing aspect of this trend is that these failures occur in spite of a rise in institutionalized examination fraud and malpractice. There are *'special centres'* for malpractice where the students pay for access to answers to examination questions. Some even have the examinations written for them by mercenaries. Advances in digital communication technology have also added more sophistication to examination fraud. Students photograph examination questions and send to their contacts outside the examination hall. Completed answers are subsequently sent by their mercenaries through the short message services (SMS). Despite these, the results are still very poor. One can only imagine what the real result would be like without examination malpractice.

The most disheartening dimension to this unfortunate situation is that most of these students that indulge in malpractices make bold to narrate how they copied in the examination halls. I met a girl in a cybercafé in Abuja in April 2012; she checked her JAMB result on the JAMB website and scored 208. She was so happy that it was above the benchmark 200. So I said to her, well, she would need to do a lot better in post-University Matriculation Examination (post-UME) so as to push it up. To my greatest surprise and consternation, this girl boldly narrated how she outmanoeuvred the invigilators in the examination hall to get her answers from her mercenaries outside the hall. I was so scandalized that the girl was proud to have scored only 208 on a scale of 400 despite the fraud.

The fact that many students now see examination malpractice as normal is worrisome. That is the same mentality they carry into the higher institutions, which also leads to producing half-baked graduates. That is the reason more than two-thirds of the graduates are in the category of second-class lower divisions, third class and pass notwithstanding the increase in malpractice at all levels.

It is not difficult to establish a correlation between the quality of knowledge imparted on products of our primary and secondary educational systems and the results of the candidates in standardized examinations like Common Entrance Examinations, the West African School Certificate (WASC) Examinations, the National Examination Council (NECO) Examinations and the Joint Admissions Matriculation Board (JAMB) Examinations. The continued poor performance of students at these examinations as shown above is indicative of poor quality of instruction at the primary and secondary educational system. In early 2013 when I travelled to my town, I went through my nephew's school report card and shockingly read his teacher's remark: 'He have to work harder'. Some teachers employed in the private and public schools are not qualified to teach, they ought to be taught. As regards to the quality of knowledge imparted on graduates of tertiary institutions in Nigeria, it is quite a different matter because of the time lag between graduation and the detection of the problems of standards in the products of higher institutions in Nigeria. The first real indication of the quality of Nigerian graduates comes from the employers of labour only when even the shortlisted 'best candidates' for employment begin to display traits that clearly cannot be those of first-rate products.[21] Increasingly, even the best products of our tertiary institutions have to undergo substantial retaining by employers before they can become productive.[22]

Abdulkarim Norde Bello[23] in his contribution 'Falling Standards of Education in Nigeria: Who Is to Blame?' identified the issues of discipline, automatic promotion of students, inadequate attendance, absenteeism, lateness to classes, lack of adequate punishment in schools, unruliness, the quest for paper qualification, and politics of admission as among the probable causes of this decline. Discipline, that system of rules, punishments, and behavioural strategies appropriate to the regulation of children or adolescences and the maintenance of order in schools, is completely lacking or has declined considerably. He identified discipline as one of the outstanding attributes of education when it is rightly observed. He also observed that students are nowadays promoted automatically, irrespective of their level of academic performance. Schools no longer insist that poorly performing student should repeat until they have gained enough knowledge to move to the next level. He insists that the 75% of attendance universally accepted as the threshold for students to sit for examination is no longer observed. Students that are late to school or classes are no longer punished. Likewise, students are no longer punished for misbehaviour for fear of reprisal action (loss of jobs or unnecessary transfer) by their affluent parents or, in the peculiar case of private schools, fear of withdrawing their wards from the school. The existence and entrenchment of gangsterism in schools, usually referred to as cultism in Nigeria, distracts students from academic pursuits. This situation persists in part due to wrong admissions policies not based on merits. Finally, the politics of admission into institutions over time ensures that schools can no longer set targets for admission concomitant to their facilities as powerful political forces ensure that the school authorities either admit students above their infrastructure and instruction capacity of the schools.

Apparently, there is serious problem in the education system. Most stakeholders are not playing their part. In my mind, the student has the greatest blame as he can actually help himself or herself. Students are not doing what they need to do. Most students do not read anymore because they believe they can always get around it in the examination hall. Many students preparing for these examinations go into the examination completely devoid of any iota of information and knowledge required to pass an examination. This is because the system offers them the opportunity of indulging in all manners and forms of malpractice in the hall. Some secondary schools, tagged special centres, actually collect money from the students to provide them answers in the examination halls, especially during external examinations like WAEC and NECO. This trend starts from the secondary schools and continues to the higher institutions. The result: production of stark illiterates.

This background now takes us to the main issue of discussion: How does the student help himself despite all these teething problems? What are the hands-on tips and practical solution available to the student to achieve academic excellence in the midst of this level of fallen standards?

CHAPTER TWO

Be Focused

Firmness of purpose is one of the most necessary sinews of character, and one of the best instruments of success. Without it genius wastes its efforts in a maze of inconsistencies.[24]

—Lord Chesterfield, 3rd Earl of Chesterfield (1694-1773)

A *'focused mind power is one of the strongest forces on earth'*,[25] says an American inspirational and motivational speaker and a founder and co-creator of the Chicken Soup for the Soul book series, Mark Victor Hansen. Focus means concentrating, looking ahead, and keeping your attention on something. It is the key to success. Distractions abound in school. Many issues vie for the attention of the student, but the only way to overcome these distractions is to remain focused.

Being focused connotes having a dream, goal, vision, or something that you aim to achieve in the future. Your goal is the end result of your action. Before embarking on something, you need to define ahead of time what you really aim to achieve. Remember that it is only goal setters that are goal getters. *Helen Keller was once asked if there was anything worse than losing one's sight. She responded, 'Yes, losing one's vision.'* [26] *'Without goals, and plans to reach them, you are like a ship that has set to sail with no destination,'*[27] says world-famous psychologist, lecturer, and writer Fitzhugh Dodson (1923-1993). John Foster (1888-1959), a former US secretary, said, *'It is a poor disgraceful thing not to be able to reply with some certainty to the simple questions, what you will be? What will you do?'*[28] Dr Charles added that *'peak performers are people who are committed to a compelling mission. It is very clear that they care deeply about what they do and their efforts, energies and enthusiasms are traceable back to that particular mission.'*[29]

Setting Goals

Goal setting is a *sine qua non* for any individual that really wants to get somewhere at some specific period in the future. Its necessity is also evident by the fact that all sophisticated organizations do map out their visions and missions at the inception of their businesses. This enables them to remain focused, rather than dissipate their energy and resources on activities that do not contribute to their reason of being in existence. So every serious student needs to be very precise as to the reason for being in school. If not, like Maurice Witzer said, '*You seldom get what you go after unless you know in advance what you want.*'[30] Its importance informed why Paul the Apostle said, '*This one thing I do . . . I press towards the mark of the high calling.*'[31] If you have no benchmark, tell me what would you press toward? Nothing!

Lack of focus can be likened to a driver on the highway who is looking sideways and behind instead of looking forward. Certainly he will crash sooner than later! Being focused drives absolute personal responsibility. Your friend or parents cannot stay focused on your behalf, you must do it yourself. What you set your heart on will determine how you will spend your life. You need to set an academic goal for yourself. By so doing, you eliminate distractions. *'Goals are new, forward-moving objectives. They magnetize you towards them. It's time to stop tiptoeing around the pool and jump into the deep end, head first. It's time to think big, want more and achieve it all,'*[32] remarked Mark Victor Hansen.

For instance, a goalkeeper can only catch a ball if he is focused on catching it. Goals of what you want to achieve, visions of great academic prowess, and dreams of being relevant across the globe are great at keeping you focused in your academic work. Carl Sandberg, an American writer, editor, and poet (1878-1967), said, *'There are people who want to be everywhere at once and they get nowhere.'*[33]

How Can You Get What You Want in Your Academics?

William Locke answered, *'I can tell how to get what you want; you have just got to keep a thing in view and go for it, and never let your eyes wander to the right or left or up or down. And looking back is fatal.'* [34] Mark Victor Hansen also affirmed that *'with vision, every person, organization and country can flourish'.*[35] The Bible says, 'Without vision we perish.' Bear in mind that if you chase two rabbits at once, the two will escape! Concentrate on what you are doing while you are at it. The more complicated you are, the more ineffective you will become. Focus on your academic work and eliminate other engagements that might dissipate your academic strength and efforts. *'This one step—choosing a goal and sticking to it—changes everything,'* [36] says Scott Reed.

> **The Big Questions**
> - What do I want in life?
> - Why am I in school?
> - What do I want to achieve?
> - Where do I want to be in the future?
> - What do I intend to make out of what I am doing?
> - How do I want to be seen in the future?
> - How do I want my parents to see and feel about me?
> - What do I want my siblings to say about me?
> - What do I want my children to say about me?
> - What impact do I want to make in my community, state, nation, continent and the world at large?
> - What do I want to be remembered for?
> - Will I be proud of the outcome of my actions tomorrow?
> - Am I working hard enough to facilitate achievement of my dreams, targets, goals, and expectations?

Have a Plan

For effective goal setting, Rick Hansen, a Canadian Paralympian, advised that *'the goal you set must be challenging. At the same time, it should be realistic and attainable, not impossible to reach. It should be challenging enough to make you stretch, but not so far that you break'.*[37] This is followed by commitment moment, which is a time to commit yourself to your target. This commitment can only be distinct when you have a plan since planning is a crucial step for success and vital for excellence. A defining moment for a trailblazer is when he takes time to plan his action instead of just reacting to daily tactical demands. *The shortest avenue or channel from where you are to the place where you would like to be is* ***'a plan'***. You really need to set a high-definition vision for yourself. To do that effectively, you need to ask yourself some BIG questions. These questions will help you define your focus as Anthony Robbins affirmed that *'quality questions create a quality life. Successful people ask better questions, and as a result, they get better answers'.*[38] Do not be fast in answering them, take it bit by bit (see box above).

With appropriate answers to these questions, you have a defined goal. You must ensure that your goal is **SMART**, which means as follows:

S	**The goal must be Specific**: Your set goal must be something precise. You should not make vague statements, like, 'Okay, I want to pass well in my examinations'. The word **well** is relative, so you should state clearly, 'I want to make nine As this term. I want my grade point average to be above 4.78 this session.' Be exact about your goal!
M	**It must be Measurable**: Such statements as 'I want to improve in my academic performance' without a means of measuring the extent of the improvement is not likely to lead you very far. A good way of measuring your goal is by comparing your academic grades between the current and the previous terms or semesters.
A	**It must be Attainable**: Being attainable does not mean being cheap. It does not imply that you should dream small or aim low. It means that it should be achievable given the right effort and commensurate hard work.
R	**It must be Realistic**: That your goal should be realistic does not imply being just cheap and simple. The world is ruled by men and women with dreams and visions that seem unrealistic to the ordinary person, but at the end, they make it real. Setting a goal of being the best in your class or being the overall best in your school, district, region, state, etc., or scoring 5 in a score scale of 0-5 points in a semester and even a session is possible, so it is real. People have achieved that and so can you. Scoring all As in a semester is real. Scoring 100% is possible but may not seem realistic to a mediocre.
T	**It must have a Time limit**: This means specific time for achieving the said goal. It is better to divide the main goal into smaller components with specific time of accomplishing each. For instance, you want to make an A in a subject/course and you plan to read some texts in preparation for the exam. You need to finish a given number of chapters or texts before the examination starts. It is not sufficient to just say 'I will read these textbooks'. This is very vague. You might end up not opening any of the texts, or actually get started but do not finish any. But when your goal is to read at least one chapter daily from the beginning of the semester, you will try to stick to that because it is time-bound.

These will help you in shaping your way of life, the activities you engage in, and how you spend your time not only in school but in general life pursuit. Mark Victor Hansen supports this when he said, *'By recording your dreams and goals on paper, you set in motion the process of becoming the person you most want to be.'* [39]

Focus is the primary thing just as Lord Chesterfield opined, *'Firmness of purpose is one of the best instruments of success. Without it, genius wastes its efforts in a maze of inconsistencies.'* [40] Ronald Reagan, a two-term president of the United States (1981-1989), informed us, *'My philosophy of life is that if we make up our mind about what we are going to make of our lives, then work hard toward that goal, we never lose—somehow we win out.'* [41] The fact remains, according to Dan Dierdorf, an American football player and television sportscaster, that *'if I've got correct goals, and if I keep pursuing them the best way I know how, everything falls into line. If I do the right thing right, I'm going to succeed.'* [42]

In line with a wise saying, you are advised to *'be a postage stamp, stick to one thing (your academic work especially in your school days) till you get there (get to the top of the ladder of academic excellence)'.* [43] Remember, you can still do whatever you think you need to divide your study time with when you are through with school, but your years in school are numbered.

'Our goals', according to Andrew Carnegie, *'must be able to command our thoughts, liberate our energy and inspire our hope.'* [44]

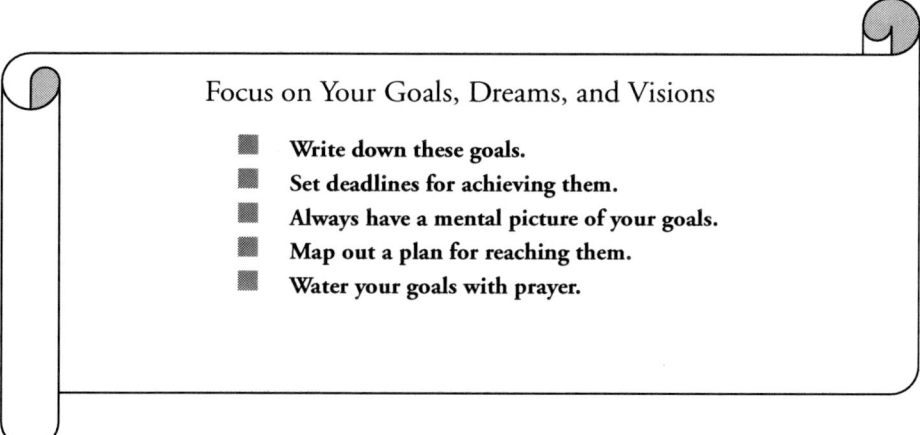

Focus on Your Goals, Dreams, and Visions
- **Write down these goals.**
- **Set deadlines for achieving them.**
- **Always have a mental picture of your goals.**
- **Map out a plan for reaching them.**
- **Water your goals with prayer.**

Write down your academic goals and their time limits here. While you do that, remember the words of Napoleon Hill (1883-1970), an American author and the author of *Think and Grow Rich*, *'There is one quality which one must possess to win, and that is definiteness of purpose, the knowledge of what one wants, and a burning desire to possess it.'* [45] He further stated that it is paramount to *'cherish your visions and your dreams as they are the children of your soul; the blue prints of your ultimate achievements'*.[46] *'The more goals you set, the more goals you get,'* [47] says Mark Victor Hansen.

Now that you know what you want, in the next chapter, we shall have a little reflection on how your academic journey started.

CHAPTER THREE

How Did Your Academic Journey Start?

Success is not a place at which one arrives but rather the spirit with which one undertakes and continues the journey.[48]

—Alex Noble

Before you set out on a journey, you must have a destination in mind. Lao Tzu, Chinese philosopher (604 BC-531 BC) said that *'the journey of a thousand miles begins with one step'*.[49] Your academic journey started from somewhere. It might be that you started from kindergarten to primary, to secondary, and maybe now you are in the tertiary institution. You see, you actually started from somewhere! It is important to find out how it all started for you and what your attitude towards education has been over time. What was your life as a pupil like? What about as a secondary or high school student?

Were you the type that liked going to school, learning new things that would be recited for Mummy at home, curious about learning strange things, and always punctual? Were you the type that took pride in representing your school in competitions at different levels, that cared so much about emerging as the best from your primary school days and remembered to do their homework? If yes, I will categorize you as **Group A**.

Or were you the type that never liked anything school, would manufacture all forms of excuse just to stay out of school, even feign sickness just to stay at home and play, cry when forced to school, and would never be in class? Are you the type that breaks every single rule in school so as to be suspended? The type that maintained the last position in class or never cared about his or her position at the end of the term? If yes, I will categorize you as **Group B**.

This background has a lot to do with your perception of education. If you belong to Group A that always want to be on top, I am sure you would always maintain that trend. Is it not so, my friend? But if you belong to Group B, I am sure you still have traces of that in your system. Somehow you might just be lackadaisical with your education, attaching little or no importance to it. You make noise while the class is in progress. If you are in school now, you might even not really consider it so interesting because you feel so restricted and would rather be somewhere else than in school.

The truth is if you belong to Group B, there are still a lot of opportunities for you to make a turnaround now. You still have the opportunity to change your perception of education and its essence. You need to appreciate the fact that *you are a student and that getting the best out of your education is your sole business at the moment.* Are you aware that there are a lot of people out there who are more intelligent, more physically endowed, and more handsome than you are but lack the opportunity of being addressed as students for once? They crave to be in your position as a student of a high school or an institution of higher learning, but to them, it can only be a dream. But here you are, wasting your time and throwing away a golden opportunity instead of expressing gratitude to God for the privilege of being a member of the elite in the academic world if you so chose.

> **FIDEAS**
> - **F**ocus
> - **I**deas (strategies)
> - **D**etermination
> - **E**fforts (hard work)
> - **A**chievements followed by
> - **S**uccess that we see now.

You might be among the group that argue and assert that it is possible to amass wealth without being educated. You may be right to some extent, but I tell you most sincerely that those you allude to often wish they had an opportunity of being educated. Many of them did not obtain any formal education, not because they did not want to, but because they never had an opportunity and the means. Some of them are even very intelligent and hardworking and would have excelled better if they had the opportunity of education. For this group, they have brought intelligence and hard work to bear on their businesses and so excelled. Getting to that level is not automatic. It took them several years of **FIDEAS** (see box).

So an unserious student who ventures into business has a higher probability of failure, as he/she is likely to embrace it with the same nonchalant attitude.

You might cite the example of Bill Gates and Steve Jobs and the few others, but the question is do you have that talent, determination, and the ability to do what they did? Each of these men, including admired names such as Edison, Mozart, the Beatles, Nadal, Michael Jackson, Warren Buffet, and Kasparov, spent no less than 10,000 focused hours on their core subject before they excelled.[50] Are you focused enough to even identify the talent in you? Do you have that zeal for hard work and perseverance? What they achieved is still very much out of cheer focus, hard work, determination, and above all, unwavering commitment. They still pressed towards the mark!

Listen to this: *'Behind every technological breakthrough there lies a dream. Behind every new product there lies a dream. Dreams create realities—through hard work,'* [51] says Rolf Jensen, the author of the *Dream Society*. It was Margaret Thatcher, a British politician, the longest-serving (1979-1990) prime minister of the United Kingdom of the twentieth century, and the only woman to have held the post, who said, *'I do not know anyone who has gotten to the top without hard work. That is the recipe. It will not always get you to the top, but it will get you pretty near.'* [52] According to J. C. Penney, *'Unless you are willing to drench yourself in your work beyond the capacity of the average man, you are just not cut out for positions at the top.'* [53] So achievements require a lot of hard work.

Those who cite examples of riches without education in Nigeria, often forget that a lot of the uneducated rich among us are not really that contented with all these wealth. Despite their wealth, a lot of them still feel inferior. Some do enrol for sandwich programmes to close the education gap. I am sure you can find examples of this in your own immediate environment. Why are these people still so much interested in getting university qualification despite all the wealth they amassed? That is the million-dollar question. Are they going to get a job with it? Why is it so important to them that they throw big parties when they acquire one? This is simply because it is a great thing to be educated! It is a landmark achievement that will always keep your head high. If you are not so sure of the importance of education, take another look at the 2011 United Nations (UN) Human Development Report on poverty and the amount of resources that is being devoted to education. It is so important. That is why every human being starts life with education at home and later in school.

You can admit as true that the rich but uneducated fellows require the services of graduates for proper running of their businesses. They need accountants to handle their finances, economists to make trade forecasts and provide advisory services, engineers and scientists to run their factories, and business managers for operational efficiency and proper management of their businesses. Without these graduates, operational efficiency will be impaired and their businesses will not operate optimally. So there is ample justification for education.

Wealth is not everything. That is not to say that wealth does not have its usefulness. It does provide for the physical needs of man but does not provide satisfaction for all needs. Wealth cannot replace education in one's life. Education empowers you and distinguishes you any time, any day. Even in antiquity, an educated person has always been held in high esteem and accorded great respect. No matter how you choose to see it, the truth remains that an educated person will always feel superior because education brings out the best in you, empowers and elevates you to an enviable position. It is only education that allows you to rub minds with the best brains all over the world. Wealth, even as important as it is, cannot give you that opportunity. You require education to compete globally. Even where an educated person decides to venture into business, his approach, organization, and management will clearly be different from that of an illiterate. You might not fully appreciate the good you are doing to yourself now by being in school, but sooner or later, it will definitely become crystal clear to you.

While I must say congratulations to you now for being a student, you need to make the best of it! That is why this book came your way! So just free your mind and feel the flow.

What Are Your Antecedents?

Where you are coming from has a lot to do with where you are going to. It can motivate you or deter you, depending on how you see it. If you start by feeling unlucky due to your background, then you are not likely to succeed. Reason: you will not even have the will or strength to try. *No matter your personal circumstance, I want you to always know right now that you are not as unfortunate as you may think.* God made you in his own image and likeness, and before you came to this world, he had charted a colourful destiny for you as in the book of Romans. Some students' academic standing is really shaped by their perception of their background. While the majority of student from the first category (see box) may strive to maintain the trail and often exceed the feats of their parents, a sad minority though may feel that their parents have achieved it all, so they need not exert themselves again. The same applies to those in the second category. Those in the third group might feel 'just there', 'let's do this and get out of here', while some will really want to reach higher by aiming at elevating the socio-economic status of

> **Where Do You Belong?**
> - Those who have educated parent(s)/sponsor with high financial standing.
> - Those who have unlearned parent(s)/sponsor with high financial standing.
> - Those who have learned parent(s)/sponsor with average financial standing.
> - Those who have unlearned parent(s)/sponsor, and also low financial standing.
> - Those who have no parents living or no steady sponsors.

their families. Those who belong to the fourth category mostly have this determination of turning things around for themselves and for their families, while some others who find themselves in that situation might not hang on for long but give up along the way. Those in the last group usually strive to better their lives by getting the best out of their education irrespective of the amount of personal suffering and sacrifice they will undergo. Sadly, only a handful of students in this category manage to reach the finishing line. These are those that believe what Tony Robbins, an author and motivational speaker said, *'The past does not equal the future.'* [54] Majority in this group drop off on the wayside. Determination is usually the key driver here. Now that you have reflected on your background and can place yourself in one of the above groups, see what the next chapter is sayng.

CHAPTER FOUR

Background Never an Obstacle

Be not afraid of greatness. Some people are born great, some achieve greatness and some have greatness thrust upon them.[55]

—William Shakespeare, English poet and playwright
(1564-1616)

'It doesn't matter where you are coming from. All that matters is where you are going,'[56] says Brian Tracy. I tell you what, your background does not determine your destination. It is your perception and determination that matter. Think about this, have you ever seen a celebration for failure? Obviously *no*! But there are always conscious or unconscious celebrations for success. Parents always pride themselves in the success of their children while their children's failure inflicts pains and hopelessness on them. But you do not strike me as a failure, so you should never be a failure. Thank God I got to talk to you through this book. Take a good look at yourself in the mirror. Come on do it! What do you see? Do you see failure or success? Yes, I believe you are looking at success! All right? Look, I want to tell you that your previous circumstance is not the determining factor of your destination. **You** can **determine** your **destination** first, and ask for **God's grace**!

Remember the saying, *'As you make your bed, so shall you lie on it.'* [57]. In academic sense, whatever your performance is will be what is attached to your name alone, not anyone else's. The certificate will not bear any other person's name except yours. I am very sure you really would love a splendid result! Great! That's why this book is here to give you some tips. Just calm down and read on with concentration so as to absorb every bit of it. It will surely help you a lot! No matter how rich and educated your parents are, you really need to define, shape, and establish your own personality. Do not relax and feel that your parents have achieved it all. You need to agree with John

Mason when he said that *'no matter how tall your father is, you have to do your own growing'*.[58] So you need to be focused and achieve even higher than your parents so your own children will take pride in you.

Imagine your certificate bearing some wonderful first-class honours degree. Just imagine it. Contrast it to the feeling you will have if your certificate is bearing a Pass degree or you are referred on some subjects and probably have an extra year to spend in school. If you are in high school, imagine you having the best result in your class and wearing a special best student badge or tie and getting all the special treatment and standing ovations at academic gatherings. Or you making the best result in your O-level examination, which automatically makes you a star, a celebrity making headlines, with many scholarship opportunities in the best higher institutions in the world. Compare that with failing and being compelled to repeat classes with your juniors or attend make-up summer school while your mates are on holidays. Or failing in your O-level examinations and having to repeat that many years on, even when your mates are graduating from higher institutions. Which would you prefer? I am sure you prefer the first one, right? Of course! I am telling you now that you can decide to change your academic biases and preferences for good. If it is good already, you make it better by blazing the same trail as your parents or doing even better. If you are the first in your family to be educated, then be the **TRAILBLAZER**! Set the trend! You can make the effort and God will strengthen you and bless your deed!

In whatever situation you find yourself, I want you to know that you can *'be the change you want to see'*.[59] How do I mean? You reach out for whatever good thing you desire and God will do the rest, provided you have faith. Let us say you desire to be in a higher institution and there is a financing constraint (it is mostly the case with achievers, they usually become great out of nothing), but you have not even passed your ordinary level (O Level), JAMB, and other entrance examinations. I can say you are not serious at all! So you need to get serious! Many students that made it to higher institutions did not get there because they have all the financial backing in the world. There got there because of their determination to attain greater heights. You should not see funding as a barrier to your education. Prepare your mind and excel in your O Level and JAMB examinations first, then that money will find you somehow. You do not need a bullion van before you get your papers right. A lot of students survive in school through various legal and moral means. Some carry on one small business or the other to keep them in school. This, however, requires a lot of humility and determination.

From my personal experience, I never saw the lack of finance as a real barrier. A lot of people see me as a scion of a very rich family, but it is only those that know me close up that are aware of my humble antecedents. If I had considered my financial background an impediment, it would not have been possible for me to be a graduate of economics today. To God be the glory.

While growing in my small family without a father figure, I so much desired to attend a higher institution. Given the very humble financial base of my family, this would have seemed a mission impossible. At my third level in the junior secondary school when I was 13, my grandma, who really brought me up, asked me to quit school as there was no money to continue my senior secondary school education. This was in spite of the fact that I devoted all my spare time and holidays to carry on petty trading even at that age. I sold groundnuts, mangoes, oil beans, and any produce I could lay my hands on. I cried and told my grandma that I must finish my senior secondary school education. I kept crying that I must continue my education despite spirited attempts by my grandma to get me to appreciate the situation. I understood my circumstance but refused to accept the part that I would quit school at 13. You could only imagine how badly I must have felt. My school then was just a public school, not even a private one. Thank God, somehow education in my state was declared 'free' and I gladly continued my senior secondary school (SS3) classes.

When I graduated from the third level of the senior secondary school, it was like I had reached the pinnacle of my academic endeavours. Pursuing a university degree seemed only like a dream that would never come true. Through someone's help, I started business of selling recharge cards, renting movies, and making calls. I really felt futureless then! But because I did not find satisfaction in my circumstance and the business, I kept praying and wishing that one day I will find myself within the walls of a university. While the situation appeared apparently hopeless, I still had this stubborn determination to resist anything that would come between me and my aspirations. Anybody who opined otherwise was automatically an enemy. With my savings from that business and help from God, my dream of getting into a higher institution eventually materialized.

So that was how it started for me. I kept doing one holiday job or the other and small business especially in my early years in the university and God blessed my deed. God never let me down and I am convinced that he will do the same for you. He provided for me both from expected and unexpected sources. I can never stop praising him! Do your part first and God will surely take care of the rest. If I told you my whole life experience in the pursuit of this education, you will marvel and glorify God Almighty. When you do your part, God will sure provide the public spirited people through whom he will complete the work. God does not do anything halfway; once he starts, he sees through. Just trust him, have faith, and *do your part*.

You see, a lot of students on campus have similar, worse or better, experiences than myself. In truth, whatever your circumstance, it is how you see the constraint or handle it that determines whether it will be a challenge or an opportunity for you. It was Friedrich Nietzsche who said, '*He who has a why can bear almost any how.*'[60] In this context, you will need to ask yourself, why do I think this problem is big enough to deprive me of a great, bright, and successful future? What I specifically want to tell you here is that whatever the problem, it is not big enough to deprive you of a wonderful future.

What are those problems you think your circumstance pose to you? Outline them below.

_____

_____

_____

You know what? They are not worth robbing you of an exquisite future at all. So strike them out! Jim Rohn is telling you this: '*If you do not design your own life plan, chances are you will fall into other people's plans, guess what they may have planned for you? Not much.*'[61] I agree with Ben Sweetland that '*success is a journey, not a destination*'.[62]

Now you know where you are coming from, the next chapter asks . . .

CHAPTER FIVE

Do You Have a Destination?

The world makes a way for the man who knows where he is going.[63]

—Ralph Waldo Emerson, American essayist, lecturer, and poet and the leader of the transcendentalist movement of the mid nineteenth century (1803-1882)

In life, people have different perceptions of the same thing. A thing might have a thousand meanings to different people. To some people, success can only occur when they have excelled. To others, they have achieved success so long as they did not fail, they are successful.

THE LADDER TO ACADEMIC EXCELLENCE

The reality is that success has two extremes and many steps between them. In a continuum, while the far right is excellence, the far left is still in the neighbourhood of failure. Your perception of success actually has tremendous impact on the kind of action you take towards its attainment. If you see success as anything other than failure, obviously in academic parlance, you will be very comfortable with an E grade (score between 40 and 45 per cent). However, if your definition of success is excellence and you are aware that nothing good comes easy, you will be motivated to carry out those activities as would enable you to achieve your dream. You will not be satisfied until you achieve your goal, which in academic sense is an A grade (score above 70 or 75 per cent) ceteris paribus.

When returning to school from holidays, your parents or guardians often exhort you to do your best to make them proud. Some students simply abandon those 'words of wisdom' at the gate of the school (tertiary or secondary). Some students simply believe and have made up their minds that A grade is not a remote possibility. These are the ones whose maximum academic achievements are Ds and never aim higher than making Ds. Such fellows will always retort with the remark, 'I de look for first-class abi first position?' meaning, 'I am not targeting a first class or first position'. Once you are aligned with the vision of this league of students on campus, you will place a ceiling on your personal academic demands. You will put in just enough effort to make your comfortable E grade or just to take the last pass position, say 20th position out of 25 students in your class. The moment this becomes your goal, you will find yourself skipping classes, finding every reason not to attend your lectures. You only attend the lectures of those teachers that make attendance compulsory and possibly be present only when the attendance list is being circulated. When you look around you, you find out that more than two-thirds of the students in your class are in the 'I am not targeting first-class league'. A good example is some students of the University of Nigeria, Nsukka (UNN), due to the institution's motto, which is 'To restore the dignity of man', often retort, 'I was not the person that lost the dignity of man that I must read to restore it.'

Students with this kind of perception or mentality hardly get very far and they are responsible for mass examination failure that is currently being experienced in the Nigerian educational sysem. The simple reason is that they target and prepare to make an E grade. When the examination questions becomes a little more challenging than their level of preparation, only those with a higher level of preparation may escape failure. Many students settle for the average; they do not seem to want to go an inch further. The box on the right provides a few questions you need to ask yourselves.

> **Questions You Must Ask Yourself**
> - Are you very proud of just an average performance?
> - Are you comfortable with being a mediocre performer?
> - Do you think that you do not need to work a little harder to achieve something better?
> - Is your current performance really your best?
> - Are you proud of it?
> - Can you proudly announce it to your parents and expect a hug from them or to your siblings and expect them to say that is my sister or brother?
> - Is mediocrity your destination?

'*Do not allow negative thinkers to influence you,*' advised Rev Fr T. Onoyima in a Sunday evening mass. I do not just believe that you are naturally dull and unintelligent.

Let's test you. Can you spell your name? Of course yes! How did you learn to do it, or were you born with it? So since you could learn it, what makes you think that you cannot learn every other thing? Just the same way you learnt to spell your name, you will learn anything you put your mind to. Would you rather say thanks to somebody that tells you to your face that you are a dunce, illiterate, and dullard? Of course you can even pick a fight with that person because you feel that you are better than that. So with this I can say that you are *deliberately underperforming in your academic endeavour purely by the choice.* So wake up and prove the person wrong now. Are you on the ladder yet? If not, get on it and start climbing! Hey, remember Zig Ziglar's words '*You cannot climb the ladder of success dressed in the costume of failure.*'[64]

Create a Mental Picture of Your Future

Create a picture of your beautiful tomorrow: an ideal career for yourself, a reputation across the globe, heading for international conferences, being sought after, etc. Picture an inspiring future for yourself, and imagine your bright future and how beautiful it could be!

Say these to yourself:

- I am intelligent; I just need to prove it!
- I can be the best student if only I work hard!
- My present performance is not the true measure of my ability!
- I am good enough for excellent grades!
- I am too young/old, beautiful/handsome, and smart for poor grades!
- I am too good to have a referral on any course!
    - I am too good to fail any subject!
    - I am too good to repeat a class!
- My past performance has nothing to do with my future!
- I must change for greater performance!
- I must be singled out from the crowd for the top!
- I must get on the ladder now and ensure that I achieve academic excellence!

Do you know that any of the under listed could be your destination just for the asking?

- You can be an authority in your discipline in the near future!
- You can be the governor of the central bank of your country!
- You can be the chairman/chairlady of international conferences!
- You can be a renowned author of bestselling books across the globe!
- You can be a shrewd researcher!
- You can be an astute scholar!
- You can be a first-class world consultant in whatever field you choose!
- You can be an astute banker if your interest is in the banking industry!
- You can be a powerful proprietor of any company of your choice with outstanding success!
- You can be sought after by the renowned companies and multinationals!
- You can own world-class schools, but you need to be world-class too! The list continues . . .

These might appear ambitious, but you can make yourself fit for them. Somehow you will not know your capability until you try. Whatever amount of time others devote to public shows and entertainment, you devote to your studies.

All you need to achieve any of these is to study!

The leaders, the most outstanding personalities in the academic world, are great readers. A look at one of Prof Chukwuma Charles Soludo's libraries will confirm this.

SECTION TWO

Ideas

CHAPTER SIX

Fresh in School

A little knowledge is a dangerous thing, knowledge in youth is wisdom in age, knowledge is silver among the poor, gold among the nobles, and a jewel among princes.

—Italian proverb

I want to draw your attention to an obvious fact: Nobody becomes a college or university student overnight. Little or no knowledge about the transition from primary to secondary and thence to a higher institution can be harmful and often result to regrets. You often hear students attribute their poor performance in the first year to ignorance. You are now in a school environment, congratulations once again! It is not easy to pass the entrance examination, be it the Common Entrance, WAEC, NECO, JAMB, post-UME, A levels, SAT, TOEFL, and the like.

You have just commenced your classes, parading yourself as a high school student or an undergraduate. But the truth is that you do not automatically transit from one academic level to the other overnight. The transition from high or secondary school to higher institution takes time and you need to adjust in many ways than one in order to become a 'real' undergraduate. You have to learn to be and behave like an undergraduate. The same applies to transition from primary to secondary school.

The freshman year in an institution of higher learning is a transitional period during which you learn how to manage yourself, to study, and to deal with many problems that you may not have had at the secondary school level. However, you do not have to spend the whole academic year learning those. If you do, it will cost you a lot. You are more likely to accumulate poor grades that will haunt you for the rest of your undergraduate days if you do not complete the transition within the shortest possible time. For you to live up to expectation right from your first year in school, you need to appreciate the following differences between studying in primary school, secondary school, or higher institution:

- **You are on your own**: At the secondary school level, you did not have your teacher sit in the same class with you as was the case in the primary school. Your minder is your form mistress/form master. At the tertiary level, you are completely on your own. There is no teacher to chaperon you.
- **Management**: At the secondary school level, you start learning how to manage certain aspects of your academic life, unlike what you have in the primary school. At the tertiary level, you have complete freedom to manage your academic pursuit, personal life, health, finances, social life, and entertainment. You are at liberty to manage these contending demands for your time in such a manner as not to encroach into your study time.
- **Study**: As a student or undergraduate, it is expected that you should to be able to study on your own, manage your time, choose your courses, preview and review your coursework or scheme of work, prepare for tests and examinations, and find help when you need one.
- **Offer more courses**: You take more courses in the secondary school and even broader courses in higher institutions. You also have more study materials to read.
- **Research**: You are also expected to learn more outside the classroom by reading your textbooks, notes, and carrying out your assignments, as well as gathering information from other sources including the internet, establishments, media, library, and the like to write term papers, academic projects, and researches.
- **Tackle Problems**: You are required to deal with many problems on your own and be able to work with other people, maybe in a group.
- **Skills**: You need to be prepared to learn not only the course, but universal skills as well.
- **Cooperation**: You have to live, co-exist, and cooperate with others who are like strangers in a new environment, including the hostel where applicable.
- **Hard work**: You simply need to be prepared to work hard.

With these things in mind, you will find adaption to your new life easy. For a good number of students, the lack of preparedness to effectively deal with these new and often competing demands and expectations of the college or university environment away from their home lies the foundation for their ensuing academic difficulties. When they get overwhelmed at this early stage and lack the ability to personally guide themselves or the opportunity to be guided by others on how to cope with or survive this persistent cycle of physical, psychological, and mental pressure, they accept defeat as a way of life and end up performing very poorly academically.

Again, many students do not have the required academic work ethics. This means that they do nothing serious outside the classroom, and they often choose other extra-curricular activities over their class attendance and academic work. They choose more of social activities over reading their textbooks and doing their classwork. The simple reason for this is that students from this category lack the self-discipline and sense of responsibility and focus to guide or drive them out of the cloud. Some people keep wallowing in this cloud until it is too late to make a visible change. If you are in this category, *now* is the time to change. Les Brown remarked that *'we cannot achieve what we have never achieved before until we become whom we have never become before'*.[65] I tell you, if you have this kind of problem or challenge and you are reading this book now, you are on the path of victory, as the book will provide you with the hands-on guide to rediscovering yourself. If you are a freshman and you encounter this kind of readjustment and realignment problem, calm down, take a deep breath, and read on, you are now closer to solving your problems.

What are the changes you need to make now to get climbing on the academic ladder of excellence?

_____

_____

_____

Get to work now! Start working from your first year. Get on that ladder now!

CHAPTER SEVEN

Failure as a Result of Obstacles

Getting an idea should be like sitting down on a pin. It should make you jump up and do something.[66]

—E. L. Simpson

In an academic environment, the end result of the many obstacles students face is *failure*. To throw more light on what I am saying here, let us explore *a few definitions of academic failure*.

The very concept of academic failure varies in its definition. Rodriguez Castellanos (1986) considers academic failure as the situation in which the subject does not attain the expected achievement according to his or her abilities, resulting in an altered personality that affects all other aspects of life. Similarly, Tapia (2002) opines that, while the current educational system perceives that the student fails if he or she does not pass, more appropriate for determining academic failure is whether the student performs to his or her potential. This might be taken to mean failure to achieve the academic target.

It is common to hear students saying 'I studied so hard for this exam and I still only got a low grade. What should I do?' Many students feel so frustrated because to them, they did what they knew was right, but the payoff was not encouraging after all. This kind of academic failure is mainly caused by a deficit in foundational learning skills. A solid foundation is very necessary. For instance, to be a good football player, you will first of all master the foundational skills like dribbling and heading the ball. To be able to learn, one needs to master the foundational learning skills, like the ability to concentrate, remember and think logically, present convincingly, and the like.

Betty J. Cappella, Marion Wagner, and Julia A. Kusmierz in a 1982 study[67] observed that there is a strong correlation between study attitude and academic performance. Academic failure can be attributed to poor study habits, poor memory, lack of motivation, fear of responsibility that follows success, lack of confidence, test and exam anxiety, lack of vision, lack of good organizational skills, peer pressure, lack of discipline, lack of passion (for a specific career goal), procrastination, and the like. There are many other factors that could facilitate academic failure, some of them are from our relationships, our environments, and others are personal attitudes as would be explored in the next three chapters.

Academic failure generally results in littering the nation with half-baked graduates in every field of study. For you that are reading this book, are you (going to be) part of this pack of ill-educated graduates? People in your field are making positive headlines. Why can you not do even better? Have you witnessed a smart and intelligent, well-read lawyer in a court before? That can make you fall in love with the legal profession. What about an outstanding medical doctor, a specialist in his field, the likes of Ben Carson, a neurosurgeon who did what his teachers even thought was impossible? Then you will love the medical profession. A foreign language student who is fluent in the languages will make you want to be a linguist. What about such outstanding and world-sought-after economists likes Dr Ngozi Okonjo Iweala? There is glory that comes with excellence in whatever field you persevere in. Academic failure is disheartening, not just to the individual, but also the people around him.

Let me highlight some unsavoury aspects of academic failure in our society today. A less-than-diligent medical student can never make a good medical doctor; even where he manages to qualify as a doctor, the same attitude will be carried in his professional practice. He will never update his knowledge and skills. Sooner than later, he becomes a quack with attendant high mortality and poor quality service in any hospital under his/her care. The unacceptable rise in the amount spent by Nigerians on medical tourism yearly attests to the fact that well-to-do Nigerians do not trust the medical practice in the country. The problem I believe is not just that of inadequate equipment, but also that of uncompetitive and poorly equipped and motivated medical force. Many medical students do not know all they ought to due to academic laziness. Some feel they cannot cope with the demands but choose to practice just because their parents want to be addressed as parents of medical doctors (Mama and Papa Doctor). Similarly, an engineer who cannot function as a professional will find himself seeking for job in a bank as a transaction officer. Examples abound.

Academic failure disorganizes and frustrates one. It breeds nothing satisfying. The sponsor of a poorly performing student would regard money spent on the student as a waste of resources. Academic failure deprives one of the opportunity of attaining enviable positions in their fields of endeavour. A person who passes his /her examination through crooked means will always be a source of disgrace to himself, his family, or any organization that has the misfortune of employing him.

CHAPTER EIGHT

Relationship-Related Obstacles

Associate with men of good quality if you esteem your own reputation; for it is better to be alone than in a bad company.[68]

—George Washington (1731-1799), first president of the United States of America

People's behaviour, output, or performance is usually influenced, affected, or even determined by their psychological, mental, or emotional state of mind, among other factors. The student's psychological state has a lot to do with their academic performance and concentration. Our emotional well-being goes a long way in determining how efficient we can be in whatever we do. When one is emotionally, psychologically, and mentally stable, there is that tendency to perform better than when one is emotionally stressed, traumatized, and disturbed. Many students under-achieve in their academic work because of the different categories of stress they undergo emotionally. These emotional stresses could be family-induced, friends-induced, relationship-induced, environmental, and the like.

RELATIONSHIP-RELATED OBSTACLES

Family-Induced Stress

Family conditions rank highest among the other factors that induce stress for the student. Most parents in contemporary times unknowingly and unintentionally cause their children or ward a lot of emotional agony. When there is lack of love in the family, between the husband and the wife, when they exhibit callousness towards each other, the children would hardly be stable emotionally and this will invariably be transferred to their performance. They can hardly concentrate in whatever they do. Look at it this way. Imagine a family where there is love lost between the parents (see picture above); it is only natural that this state of affairs will be transferred to the children. The children from this type of dysfunctional family, where the parents are constantly at war with each other, quarrelling, fighting, and exhibiting great meanness, generally feel alienated both in their family and in the larger society. This kind of parents hardly pay attention to their children to teach them what they should know and give them proper guide in their academic work, possibly answer their questions and understand their needs. In this kind of family, the children do not even know what it feels like to be loved. They are always in a chartered emotional state. They keep feeling bad and wishing they were not born in such families. They feel deserted and often crave for a peaceful and loving home. They always dream and wish they had a more loving, comfortable, and caring family. Students under this condition most times underperform in whatever they do because they are always absent-minded. They lack the drive and motivation to perform. They have nobody they really want to impress with good performance. They are usually psychologically unbalanced and defeated. In fact, sometimes children in this category may even intentionally under-achieve in protest just to punish their parents who they see as uncaring.

On the contrary, in a family where love exists (see picture above), the children will always feel cherished by their parents, they always feel the love of their parents for them and for each other, and so strive to make their parents proud and happy. They will delight in striving to achieve what will always endear them to their parents. You see the impact of love in the family?

My Advice

My little advice for such parents is to always try a little introspection and assess the potential impact of their unloving dispositions on their children and their future. They should at least, for the sake of the children, better manage their differences and handle problems maturely like good parents so as to maintain a stable, loving, peaceful, and caring home, which will be a place of pride, a centre of attraction, and a real home to their children, not just a house. They should try and be good role models to their children as this tends to elicit the best from the children. A little loving encouragement to your child with a pat on the back will always encourage the child to earn their parent's respect. Virginia M. Shiller, an author, said, *'It is essential as parents to help our children see the benefits inherent in doing the right thing. By reinforcing your child's good behavior, you will help him understand the rewards that good behavior brings.'* [69] Parents, please maintain closeness to your children and teach them with love.

To the children, losing interest in your academics as a protest to your parents' attitude is not in your best interest. You might think you are punishing them, but believe me, you are doing yourself and your future a lot more harm. This could be likened to biting the nose to spite the face. You are just burning your own house in the bid to chase a rat. If you find yourself in this type of situation, always see yourself as the very agent of change. See yourself as the person that can turn the bad situations around you, including stabilizing your home. But to command such respect, you need to be focused and study for a brighter future, thereby empowering yourself to be the change you desire. Wallowing in self-pity will never get you these. Through hard work and academic achievement, you can turn around a lot of situations around you including your home for the better. Do not keep hiding under the dysfunctional behaviour of your parents as a reason for underperformance. Just take it as one of the challenges in life and work towards resolving it. Picture yourself in a very good position in the near future. Select a role model or models in your field and work hard to attain their status or even surpass their achievement. Envision a future for yourself like that of your role model. How does it feel? It sure feels great! Then you talk to your parents, I assure you that they will listen to you and try to make amends. So get that empowerment you require first by getting the best out of your academics now. Okay? Do not be deterred at all. Some people had even worse experiences and conditions but still emerged successfully as heroes. President Barack Obama is a good point of reference. So join their league. You are a potential star!

Friends-Induced Stress

The attachment to our friends and peers also has a lot to do with our emotional stability. We are usually more stable when the going is good but depressed when the going turns sour. It is often the case that when we get so attached to some persons as our friends, we tend to mirror their behaviour. When we are happy with our dear friends, we are at peace. We see them as sources of encouragement and inspiration in our lives. Sometimes we get so entangled that we develop this feeling of their indispensability in our lives. They become an integral part of our lives. So how students relate to their friends actually play a great part in determining their performance in everything they do, including their academic work. Some people get so attached to their friends that they cannot function as individuals without their support, tele-guidance, and influence on any issue, including their attention to academic work.

Advice

My advice here is that the level of attention and devotion to friendship should depend primarily on the extent to which the relationship is instrumental to the achievement of your academic goals. *Foster* good friendships if they support your academic objectives, but *discard* them if they draw you back. This exhortation is also relevant even for any type of relationship, where one can get deeply attached to persons who have little respect for one's values, welfare, and the like. Just maintain acquaintances, at least, for now so your academic work will not suffer.

Relationship-Induced Stress

RELATIONSHIP-RELATED OBSTACLES

Another vital aspect of emotional stress stems from the intimate relationships we find ourselves in. Intimacy can be soothing, but can also be very stressful and may even be disastrous. When people get involved intimately, they tend to give their whole heart to the partner. If and when the going gets bad, as they often do along the line, the person involved is thrown into great emotional trauma and turmoil that often affects every facet of the person's life. This is true for most people.

A good example is a superior in an office who was annoyed by the spouse before coming to work. No matter how strong that person is, the accompanying emotional disequilibrium will likely affect their activities, disposition, utterances, and behaviour at work. He or she will not be at their best, and their performance will be suboptimal. It generally affects their whole being. Friends will generally find them irritating as such times.

Let us now narrow this down to the student. When they get involved in a romantic relationship, many get carried away and oftentimes lose focus of what is required of them academically. Problems in that relationship are often accompanied by unhappiness, distress, and inability to concentrate. They have little motivation to carry on constructively, including attending classes and reading. It takes a long time to stabilize. Sometimes this might happen during examinations or close to the examination period. The consequence could be grave. It oftentimes leads to poor academic performance in the semester/term in question. So a romantic relationship is one of the greatest distractions that students face in school that results in poor academic performance. The question now is, are you caught up in this web?

My Advice

My advice here is this, I cannot assure you of a perfect relationship since human beings are meant to have and settle problems. However, if you are not emotionally mature to handle romantic friendship or relationship-related stress, the best choice is to do without it in your school days. You can do that all your life after school. But if you must indulge in one, get someone with whom you share some personal aspirations, someone that will not want to hurt you, somebody that is sensitive and may be sympathetic to your dispositions and emotions and cares about your academic performance. I don't mean someone you think does, but someone you are sure of. Don't be deceived.

The People You Mix With and Peer Negative Influence

'Look around your environment; what kind of people are there? What kind of language do they speak? what do they believe, what are their thoughts, dreams, direction, values in life, what are their guiding philosophies and what especially are their goals?' asked Chidi Okpaluba.[70] Take a mental look at the people you associate with daily. In some peer groups, being smart is despised and these groups tend to share collective low aspirations even in their academic work. At your youth, it is in your interest not to engage in risky, self-destructive behaviours, including those that will destroy your future. But many young people do not care about this. Many see the time in higher institutions or secondary school dormitory as opportunity to explore the world of maximum pleasure, even the very destructive. They indulge in drugs and hard substances, join violent immoral gangs otherwise referred to as cults, and embark on destructive adventurism. When your peer have this negative ideology and lifestyles, you are unlikely to escape its consequences. So it is either you stick with them and their ideologies and go down with them, or you try to change their ideology or better still, quit if they refuse to change for good.

My Avice

Are your peers the type that shows great interest in their academic work, always looking for genuine ways of improvement? Great to have this kind of friends! Or are they the type that are never concerned about their academic work, the type that display a lackadaisical attitude towards academic matters, that do not care about or take interest in what happens in class, their assignments, tests, and examinations? The type that are only attracted to the hottest parties in town, do not give a hoot to what grade they graduate with? Any grade is just okay for them? If you mix with these types of characters, monumental failure rather than academic success is likely to be your reward. I am pleading with you now to please make a very big and sharp turnaround, unless you are okay where you are, but I am convinced you are not. These characters are dream killers! See how the transmission works. If you 'buy into' the thoughts and ideas of those people surrounding you, their 'it does not matter' beliefs, you may end up creating your own negative mental image or 'it does not matter' attitude. I am positive that if you have motivated and motivating friends, you will be motivated and challenged each time you chat with them. Am I right or wrong? Of course I am right! The holy book in Corinthians 15:33 admonishes *'do not be fools, bad companions ruin good character'*.

> **Dealing With the Peer Negative Influence**
> - You need to be assertive (demand for your rights confidently).
> - You can also break away from such people.
> - In case this leads to threat, report to the security department of your school.
> - Keep only friends who are hardworking, well-behaved, ambitious, honest, obedient, and disciplined students.
> - Keep friends that are trustworthy, reliable, and contented students.
> - Avoid drug addicts and cult members.
> - Most importantly, always remember the warnings given to you by your parents or guardians.
> - You can also seek guidance from decent senior fellows in your department or your academic adviser.

The unmotivated associates will give you the wrong impression that you do not need a good result to succeed in anything. They will insist that you are just not good enough or possess the capability to achieve higher results in your academics. So there is no need to bother with academic work.

Stick with this negativity for too long, and you will invariably have very low personal esteem that will ultimately stymie your ability to dream big. See, *'if you surround yourself with the good and righteous, they can only raise you up. If you surround yourself with the others, they will drag you down into the doldrums of mediocrity, and they will keep you there, but only as long as you permit it'*,[71] so insists Mark Glamack.

I have this encouraging piece for you. It is not yet too late if you start adjusting now. Bear in mind that all ordinary people can achieve extraordinary results if they can throw away the limiting beliefs that are blocking their minds unconsciously. After reading this book, you will be able to knock this off your head and go for your 'right'. Remember the proverb that *'if you cannot beat them, you join them'*.[72] My advice for you here is to watch your group of friends. Select your friends! If you cannot change or influence them, leave them.

We will look at environmentally induced obstacles to academic performance in the next chapter.

CHAPTER NINE

Environment-Induced Obstacles

Be careful the environment you choose for it will shape you; be careful the friends you choose for you will become like them.[73]

—W. Clement Stone, author and philanthropist
(1902-2002)

Influence of Roommates

In a school environment, secondary or tertiary, students spend most of their time with their roommates. These roommates can substantially influence a student's academic performance, behaviour, and way of life. Roommates exert a lot of influence on their fellow roommates. This influence can be positive or negative. Since in most schools students do not have a choice or influence over who may or may not stay with them as roommates, everybody resigns to mother luck in this regard. It happens that sometimes one might be very fortunate to have the serious-minded types as roommates. I refer to those set of roommates usually referred to as JACKO (bookworm) at the University of Nigeria, Nsukka (UNN). As a co-occupant of this kind of room, one would not want to be the odd man out, so the best thing here is to join the reading league.

I had a friend who studied electronic engineering at the University of Nigeria, Nsukka. In her second year, she happened to be the most senior in her room in terms of academic level. So she convinced her roommates and they made it a kind of room regulation that they would study for a certain number of hours every night before retiring to bed. I guess you might have issues with this. You might ask, did she bring me to school? Is she paying my fees? What kind of controller, supervisor, or monitor is this? Why should I do that? But I tell you this helped every member of that room. They all

ENVIRONMENT-INDUCED OBSTACLES

improved in their academic work in their different courses, and my friend achieved her own academic goal that session! She eventually graduated with a first-class honours degree in electronics engineering in 2012.

Do you doubt such things? I challenge you to give it a sincere trial and see for yourself the great magic it can work! What I am saying here is that when a non-serious student gets into a room filled with the serious ones, the person will unconsciously improve in his or her academic pursuit. Remember the popular proverb *'You can lead a horse to water but you can't make it drink'*.

On the other hand, you might also be so unlucky to be thrown into a room where you have only the kind of students that have all kinds of other priorities except academic work in their calendar. These priorities might be partying, clubbing, gossiping, travelling, prostituting, flirting, terrorism, indulging in gang activities, etc.

These kinds of roommates can actually kill the morale in you if care is not taken. They will always make the room very uncomfortable for reading. If you request for less noise, they will tell you that you all paid the same amount and so have the right to do whatever you please. Most times, a lot of students under-achieve academically because of this kind of environment over which they have little or no control.

Bear it in mind that when you get into such rooms, they will do all in their power to discourage you and drag you down. They will criticize you a lot and, in negative allusion to the motto of UNN, ask you questions like 'You are reading to restore the dignity of man, were you the person that lost it?' They will even tell you that if they read like you do, they will make better grade than you or other such unhelpful comments. They will tell you that they do not read yet they pass. In this case, dear, just remind yourself that there are different grades of passing. Grades A and E are not the same and can never be. Remind yourself that you will not be comfortable with just an E grade. So you need to work for that grade that will always enable you to keep your head up, that grade that will be instrumental to that successful life you envision for the future.

You must constantly ask yourself such questions as: Who am I around with? What are they doing to me? What have they got me reading? What have they got me saying? Where do they have me going? What have do they got me thinking? And most important, what are they having me become? Then ask yourself the big question: Is that okay?

Always remember that *'your life does not get better by chance, it gets better by change'*,[74] remarked Jim Rohn. If you are the type that is motivated for something serious; something that will make you happy in the future; something that whenever and wherever you will be grateful to God that by his grace you achieved it; something that at any time anywhere you will be proud you did; something that your relations, friends, and children will be proud that you did; something that your community, nation, and humanity will always make reference to, print on the sand of history that can hardly be erased; something that will be a motivating factor for millions of people in the future; and the like, *you must not allow yourself or your academic life to be determined, overwhelmed, derailed, corrupted, or disoriented by bad, unserious, and unfocused roommates if you are unlucky to meet any such person(s) in your academic journey.* Do not jump on the *bandwagon of the Joneses!*[75]

'A strong successful man is not the victim of his environment. He creates favourable conditions,' [76] so says Orsen Marden. Just get prepared and

equipped for such a challenge so that if it throws up itself, you will not be taken unawares.

I am asking you now, to which groups of roommate do you belong, *the motivation killers* or *the motivation builders*? Ask yourself this personal question, 'Considering my attitude as a roommate, am I really a solution or a problem, a source of encouragement or discouragement to myself and others?' In answering the question, please try to adjust for the better in your own interest and that of others.

Influence of the Wannabes

Another major problem students face in the school environment that tends to stymie academic well-being is the so-called 'wannabes'. Who are these wannabes really? According to Urbandictionary.com, 'a wannabe is a poser, follower, a charlatan of sorts. One who copies or imitates all or most of the aspects dealing with their idol. They may wish to have certain clothing, skills, vocabulary, and the like, of their idols instead of their own. Most likely a wannabe is lacking in self-confidence and is looking for guidance'.[77] Wannabes are people who want to belong to a particular social class, real or imaginary, and they try to do almost anything to maintain for the appearance of being an operator in the so-called class. In most cases, they indulge in demeaning lifestyles just to keep up with the trend or worthless goals they set for themselves. This trend might include any of the following:

- To ride the latest car in town
- To always wear the most expensive clothes, shoes, and bags (for ladies)
- To always use the latest and most expensive phones
- To appear in most social gossip column as a happening socialite
- To always wear the latest designer's perfumes and wears
- To wear the most expensive weave-on (like Indian hair, Brazilian hair, etc.)
- To eat at the most expensive joint always
- To look expensive
- To move with and be identified with contrived expensive friends and people at all cost
- The list continues

Well, I am not saying that these things are not good. The issue at stake here and the questions at hand is, can you comfortably, consistently, happily, and independently sustain that lifestyle? Even if you can, are those things really your priority at this time? Many students often do not take their financial status into consideration in aspiring to a particular lifestyle. Some even want to live more extravagantly than those that actually have the means. I want you to understand that they are two different things: *looking expensive* and *being expensive*. You only *look expensive* when you are actually not but only trying to be by outward appearance alone, while you *are expensive* when you are expensive from within, which is beyond mere physical apparels. Take a look at some of the high flyers you know who can afford anything that money can buy. You may be astonished to find out that these people do not place too much value on these items that drive most students crazy. These people not only look expensive, they have that expensive aura around them, rooted in their character, achievement, or status, and not necessarily the values of dresses and make-ups they have. For instance, Dr Ngozi Okonjo Iweala, a senior World Bank official, the coordinating minister of the economy and the minister of finance, Nigeria, the first African woman to be nominated for the much-coveted and revered World Bank presidency seat in 2012, in a program I watched on television in the middle of 2012, challenged women—she was carrying a locally made handbag (the one popularly known in Nigeria as 'Aba made'), which most students cannot even try. She has all the money to buy the most expensive Louis Vuitton, Gucci, Dolce and Gabana, and other designer handbags and wears from any part of the world, but you always see her putting on Nigerian wax. That does not diminish her fame and affluence. Think about the influential women you know, Michelle Obama, have you really looked at her well? She can afford trailers of Brazilian and Indian human hair, but that is not her problem at all. What about Dr Oby Ezekwesili, the former honourable minister for education of Nigeria and former vice president of the World Bank for Africa[78] who always wears a low cut? She said that her justification for that is that she cannot afford the time lavished on hair designing, decoration, styling, and maintenance. She can use such time and resources in better and more ennobling engagements. But today, many women in their expensive human hair and dresses line up and wait for long hours to get appointment to see her. Think about President Barack Obama of the United States, the first African to occupy the presidency of the White House twice. Examples abound. That is to show you that it is not all about the apparels. When you know your worth, then you would not indulge in most activities that classify you as a wannabe; you would not go prostituting to acquire mere consumables, which can cost you so much. It could cost you your life, your health, your destiny. Some students even indulge in armed robbery that can get one killed or even kill someone else all for frivolous reasons—to look trendy, have flashy phones, cars, dresses, date the *hottest* chicks on campus, and so on.

Sit Down and Do Some Introspection

You will see that these are not worth all the trouble! That lifestyle is too risky, filthy, and demeaning! You can never be proud of it any day! You can be a world-class player in any field of endeavour if you can just bend down and read now instead of prostituting for mere 5,000 naira or even less and submit your body that is meant to be dear and priceless to anybody that offers that change! My candid advice for you is this: you see that place you desire to get to, those things you desire to have, just calm down and do what you need to do now. You will eventually get to the position where you can have as much of them as you desire without having to go out of your way to get them. You can get to whatever position you desire, but first you need to work hard. Do the right things at the right time. Now is the time for you to study and prepare for a healthy future. A time will come when you have better things than these things that are making you do what is clearly unhealthy for you. Remember that nothing good comes easy. Make do with what you have as a student. Many students tend to overstate the importance of what they do not have. You can perform excellently without owning a BlackBerry, Android, or iPhone phone. Gadgets are very helpful for those that can actually use them to enhance their stock of knowledge, but to many other students, it is a great source of distraction and a source of failure if care is not taken. So you need to get to work now. To climb the ladder of excellence, you need to apply a force bigger than that of gravity that might be pulling you down. Brian Tracy is saying to you that *'the ability to discipline yourself to delay gratification in the short term in order to enjoy greater rewards in the long term is the indispensable prerequisite for success'.*[79]

Lack of Positive Role Models

Most students do not have anyone who they want to impress in their academic work. Having or adopting a right role model, motivator, or an inspiring figure to impress can be a very strong, positive driving force in determining a student's academic performance. Be it a mentor, a figure within the family or extended family, a public servant, a foreigner, and the like. This makes you to always struggle and work hard to meet your mentor's expectation. You unconsciously always think about your mentor's remarks or comments about your grade. You will not want to disappoint your mentor by engaging in demeaning behaviours capable of lowering our mentor's opinion of you; this is a practical reality of life. Setting high expectations for you can make you think twice before engaging in risky behaviour that might 'disappoint' your mentor. You will always be mindful of your mentor's admonition when you perform badly, so you will try to always make your mentor proud. In the case of a role model, he is driven or challenged by the dream to climb to the level of his model. A role model can make a big difference. If you have someone who wants to know your performance in school, you will sit up. The role model must be a personality you really admire!

So my advice to you is to get yourself a mentor or a role model, read about the person's life experiences, challenges, achievements, and lifestyle. This way, you will be challenged to attain even greater heights.

CHAPTER TEN

'You' As Your Own Obstacle

I do not think all failure's undeserved, and all success is merely someone's luck; Some men are down because they were unnerved, And some are up because they kept their pluck. Some men are down because they chose to shirk; some men are high because they did their work. I do not think that all the poor are good, that riches are the uniform of shame; the beggar might have conquered if he would, And that he begs, the World is not to blame. Misfortune is not all that comes to mar; Most men, themselves, have shaped things they are.[80]

—Edgar Guest, American poet (1881-1959)

Who Really Is the Obstacle?

Students often blame their failures on other people and many external factors. This is naturally very convenient, but I want to tell you that so long as you keep justifying your failure by shifting and apportioning blames to others and exonerating yourself, you will never discover the tremendous part you play in your own failure. It is possible you are the greatest enemy of yourself. Now let us examine critically this scenario and try to place issues in their practical perspectives.

I learnt from the University of Ilorin new student's guide page that tertiary institutions in Nigeria are poised fundamentally to pursue the following goals among others:

- To contribute to national development through high-level relevant manpower training
- To develop and inculcate proper values for the survival of the individual and society

- To develop the intellectual capability of individuals to understand and appreciate their local and external environments
- To acquire both physical and intellectual skills that will enable individuals to be self-reliant and useful members of the society

Specifically, university education

- frees individuals from ignorance,
- assists to develop human minds,
- prepares individuals to earn a good living,
- creates awareness about what is going on in the society and the world at large,
- enables individuals to detect their talents and to develop such talents to the fullest,
- prepares individuals to fit properly into different careers and thus promote the development of the society,
- increases the power of reasoning thus promoting scientific and technological development,
- promotes moral development of the individuals,
- enables individuals to learn and know different cultures and enhances effective interactions among people of different backgrounds,
- prepares individuals to be self-reliant,
- guides individuals to know their duties and responsibilities to the society, and
- assists in raising a generation of people who can think for themselves and respect the views and feelings of others.

The above constitute the mission of tertiary institutions in Nigeria. All stakeholders including the government, institutions, policymakers and lawmakers, teachers, parents, students, et al., are supposed to play their own specific roles and part towards achieving the above set objectives and goals.

In our country today, the jury is already out that the standard of education has fallen considerably. However, nobody, group or institution, including the stakeholders, are ready to accept responsibility for the failure. The fact remains that there is a collective failure and we stakeholders and students alike all bear some degree of responsibility. As this subject is only tangential to the focus in this book, my advice and observation is that the only workable and sustainable solution to the rot in our educational system is for each and every stakeholder to honestly identify their role in this malaise and work hard to rectify it. We have no problem of visioning or setting goals but that of poor execution, implementation, and lack of commitment and sustainability.

Now back to my focus on the students as a stakeholder. How do you as a student play your own part in ensuring that the beautiful goals articulated above are met? Do you belong to the group that keeps blaming others including the government for the entire problem?

Clearly, these goals cannot be achieved unless you, the student, play your role actively. If you keep making negative and derogatory statements, like, this school is trash, it is nothing, this school is just the worst school, they do not teach anything in this school, the teachers are bad and dullards, the standard here is poor, my question to you now is, how wonderful is your performance in the so-called bad school now? Look, if you are not currently the best student in school with poor standards, what is the likelihood of even passing in the school with the so-called better standards? Is it not possible that you currently lack the basic academic skills to excel anywhere? Possibly, you simply lack the required skill, which is *reading*. So try and prove yourself the best student in your school, Nigeria and Africa first, then we will know that you are the whiz kid and so can excel anywhere in the world. You cannot be a fulfilled student where you are now until you learn to accept the given and strive to make the best of it. Be aware that what you can do now is the only influence you have over your future. A German proverb says, *'Grow where you are planted. Begin to weave and God will give you the thread.'*

Some students go through semester/term after semester/term without any idea of what goes on in the classrooms or the content of their courses/subjects. I acknowledge that government has a big role to play by raising the standard of living of teachers and putting adequate infrastructure in place. However, infrastructure in the school environment does not impact knowledge into the student. It cannot open your brain and put your textbooks inside. You as a student have an even greater role in your quest to be a graduate. You need to ask yourself this question: what quality of graduate am I going to be after graduation? You remember the computing maxim *'Garbage in, garbage out'*? In this sense, the quality of graduate you want to be tomorrow depends on the quantum of knowledge you absorb today.

The question here is, in what ways has the student contributed to the poor quality of education in Nigeria? Remember, the standard of education is not measured by the aesthetic environment of the school alone. It depends largely on the quality of the graduates and their achievements, number of laureates received, and the like. We often place the blame only on government for the downward trend of our education system. But the question to you, the student, now is, are you sure you are not contributing more to the rot than the government? Your sincere answer to the following personal questions will be quite revealing:

- Does education mean any serious thing to you?
- Do you honestly want to be educated?
- Did you honestly earn your WAEC, NECO, and JAMB scores, or did you buy, acquire, or just receive them?
- Have you cheated in any way in any examination(s)?
- As an undergraduate, do you earn your grades or buy them with whatever resources?
- Did you get someone to impersonate for you in your examinations?
- Have you ever been a candidate of a special centre for *examination fraud*?
- If yes, why did you not take these examinations on your own?
- Do you have less ability than those that wrote theirs without any help in the examination hall?
- How much quality time do you put into your studies?
- Do you attend your classes regularly and as at when they are due?
- Do you carry out your assignment as you should?
- Do you read your recommended texts and much more?
- Have you finished reading your own textbooks, or are they mere decorations?
- Do you do enough research work with other students, explore the internet, read widely, invest in textbooks, borrow from others when you cannot afford the textbooks, and consult widely as a committed student?
- Have you ever asked yourself this question: what quality of graduate do I want to be tomorrow?

It is these issues listed above that constitute the undesirable fall in the standard of education.

So you see, you may have been a major contributor to the falling standard of education in your country! You have done this by aiding and abetting the making of low-quality graduates by ensuring through your action and inaction that the lofty goals of the tertiary institutions are not met!

What are you going to do about it? Imagine government changing all the so-called non-qualified teachers and bringing the qualified ones that teach with sophisticated texts and set more difficult questions. If you neither read nor attend classes, it will not make much difference. You (the student) are the medium through which the little efforts of government or the teachers will manifest. Without you, every effort of the other stakeholders to revive our crumbling education system will yield little or no result.

If you really want the Nigerian education system to change for good and be ranked amongst the best in the world, then you need to change your attitude towards your studies. If you have already formed the negative attitude of not reading, you need to change it. Otherwise, you will allow bad habits to chart your future to your own consternation. Like Abigail Van Buren remarked, '*It's an undo-it-yourself project.*'[81]

Having honestly answered these questions, now what is your take? Do you now consider yourself to be the cause, the victim, the casualty, or the suspect in the case of falling standard of education? Are you unwittingly an accessory to your own destruction, condemned to that group referred to as half-baked graduates?

Then this book should be an eye-opener for you. It will invariably open your eyes to your impediments and convey the simple steps you need to take with a view to turning things around for yourself and the country's education system.

CHAPTER ELEVEN

Other Individual-Related Obstacles

If you wish success in life, make perseverance your bosom friend, experience your wise counsellor, caution your elder brother and hope your guardian genius.[82]

—Joseph Addison

The following are other individual-related obstacles that can limit your academic success.

Student's Perception of Education and Its Value as an Asset

A student's perception about formal education and the measure of his faith in its ability to shape his future plays a key role in his commitment to acquiring it. For some youths/students, wealth is the end itself. People in this group are ready to sacrifice anything, including education for wealth. For such people, their role models are those rich people without formal education. For such students, being a student is just a ritual that has to be performed at a particular age. The student has no commitment and does not spend quality time in their studies. But for those who perceive education as means to the end in terms of personal achievement and their future, education is a serious business that requires the highest level of attention and commitment. Where do you belong in terms of perception of education as business or assignment? How committed are you towards pursuing the set goals or target?

Fear and Limiting Beliefs

Fear is defined by Chan in his e-book as False Evidence Appearing Real. It is the main factor that stops one from taking action even if one is motivated. Franklin Delano Roosevelt, thirty-second president of the United States

(1933-1945), said that *'the only thing we have to fear is fear itself—nameless, unreasoning, unjustified, terror which paralyzes needed efforts to convert retreat into advance'*.[83] It kills motivation irrespective of how magnificent it is. The presence of fear makes the mind focus on nothing else but on fear itself. When you experience fear, you keep feeling you cannot do it, that you might fail. It prevents you from even trying. The fear of some courses may prevent you from finding solutions to them. You keep feeling that they are too difficult for you to even try. Fear is so bad that it can make you forget the things you knew even during a test or an examination. For instance, many students are so scared of mathematical courses that they do not even try to gain just a little knowledge of them. They thus end up failing such courses.

Similarly, limiting beliefs are those imaginary beliefs that we nurture in our minds that make us see ourselves as unfit for the goal we ought to pursue. Beliefs have the power to create and the power to destroy. Human beings have the awesome ability to take any experience of their lives and create a meaning that reduces their confidence in their abilities or one that can literally save their lives. *'What we can or cannot do, what we consider possible or impossible, is rarely a function of our true capability. It is more likely a function of our beliefs about who we are,'* [84] says *Anthony Robbins*. This kind of belief blocks one's mentality and permeates one's psyche with the conviction that one cannot achieve his or her dreams. You cannot make an A grade in this or that course; you cannot be among the best students in your class. It makes you feel that you are highly incapable of achieving that. You might even start looking for reasons to justify why you cannot achieve your goals or why you are unfit. If you find yourself in this situation, the following questions will help you:

- Have you aimed high in your academic work before? If no, why?
- Did you pursue your target? If no, why?
- Have you tried pursuing your desire for academic success with the required vigour, or do you follow it lethargically?
- How do you know that such academic feat is beyond you?
- How do you know you cannot break the records in academics?
- Who and what limits your beliefs?
- Do you know that the person(s) and things influencing your belief?
- Is it the person(s) you associate with every day and the environment where you spend most of your time daily?

Okay, now that you actually have a hint of what your problems might be, the summary question now is, do you really think that there is actually a problem with your ability, or was it just a mental block? I am sure it was just a mental block. Thank God! You know you can only cure an identified disease. Is it not so, my friend? But be aware that *'the only real limitation on your abilities is the level of your desires. If you want it badly enough, there are no limits on what you can achieve',*[85] says Brian Tracy.

Procrastination

Procrastination is the habit of deferring to tomorrow what could easily have been accomplished today. According to the Encarta Dictionary, it is the act of postponement of doing something, especially as a regular practice. *'Procrastination is the art of keeping up with yesterday,'*[86] says Don Marquis, the author of *The Archy and Mehitabel*.

This is actually a major problem with a lot of students. Many a time, you hear students make comments like, 'I will start reading from the first week of the term/semester'. They will even gather materials—notebooks, textbooks, handouts, past question papers, and the like—from the senior students in a bid to start reading even before the semester/term resumes. But the *problem* is that *procrastination* never allows 98% of students to execute their plans. Even when the semester resumes, a lot of students do not resume. A lot find it difficult to read their books until the examinations are around the corner. Many students have textbooks but never open them while in school. Putting off assignments and tests for the last minute may seem a good idea for many students, but it does adversely affect their academic performance. Waiting until the last minute to carry out assignments increases the risk of failure or poor performance. Excellent assignments, homeworks, term papers, and projects go through several drafts and editing. They are rarely complete in one draft. *'Twenty years from now, you will be more disappointed for the things you did not do than by the ones you did do. So throw off the bowlines. Sail away from the safe harbor. Catch the winds in your sail. Explore. Dream,'* [87] advised Mark Twain.

Dealing with Procrastination

'We, all of us, complain of the shortness of time', says Seneca, *'and yet have much more than we know what to do with. Our lives are spent either doing*

OTHER INDIVIDUAL-RELATED OBSTACLES

nothing at all, or doing nothing to the purpose, or doing nothing that we ought to do.'[88] On the appropriate use of time, William Shakespeare said, '*I wasted time and now doth time waste me.*'[89]

A lot of big dreams and aspirations died due to procrastination. It gives you this feeling that there is still sufficient time, but before you know it, there will hardly be time. Procrastination takes its roots from laziness in humans. It, therefore, requires some efforts and determination to deal with. I had experienced this on a number of occasions. For instance, at the beginning of the semesters, I would make three to four different time tables before I would really get serious with my books. If you felt I did well after all, maybe I could have done better if I knew how to deal with procrastination then. I learnt from observation that every great man became great by proper utilization of time.

The best way to deal with procrastination is to invest your time wisely. Carolyn Castleberry exhorts us to '*track where your time goes to discover who and what is stealing your time without your permission. Keep a daily log for a few days of how much time you put into each activity in which you're involved. Then analyze the information you've written to see how much time you've spent in unexpected ways, and how much time each activity really took. After you've looked at your activities, consider how you may be wasting time emotionally, by spending time in unproductive ways like worrying and complaining. Figure out your current time management patterns, and notice how those differ from the ways you'd like to start using your time*'.[90]

The worst thing for you to do in time management is to spend your time. Any time spent can never be recouped, but it pays when you invest your time instead. Watching television is spending your time—watching others excel in their industry while you should be working to excel in your own industry (academic work).

Do you know that when you start reading early in the term/semester, you have sufficient time to read a variety of things that all go to increase your knowledge? However, if you dawdle until it is late, you can only read just to pass your examination. This way, you are most likely to saturate your brain with too much information in so short a time, information you are most likely to forget shortly after the examinations, making people doubt if you actually earned the grade you got. It happens a lot of times, but you can fight it now. Start now. Get serious. I am sure you will be proud you did. Time waits for nobody! And you cannot buy back the last minute spent no matter how rich you are. So start now! There is no reason to wait till later.

Encourage yourself to develop a schedule for studying and working on assignments. Very importantly, learn to adhere to your study plan. This not only builds time-management skills, but it also helps you to spend more time on your academic work and earning yourself better grades. Procrastination is one big problem you must tackle if you really want to be successful not only in your academic work, but also in all life endeavours. *Procrastination makes you waste valuable time, overcrowds your tomorrow, overstresses you, and at the end, undermines your output. Procrastination is a big enemy of progress!* Napoleon Hill advised, '*Do it now!* can affect every phase of your life. It can help you do the things you should do but do not feel like doing. It can keep you from procrastinating when an unpleasant duty faces you. But it can also help you do those things that you want to do. It helps you seize those precious moments that, if lost, may never be retrieved.'[91] Recall that according to Edward Young (1683-1765), a British poet, 'Procrastination is the thief of time.'[92]

Addiction to Social Networking Sites

Students who spend a lot of time watching movies invariably have less time for their studies. Some students spend as much as twenty-four hours watching movies, especially series. A lot of students have computer laptops in school, but instead of deploying the tool towards the improvement of their academic work, it becomes an accessory to poor academic performance. The same goes for students who spend all their time on social sites such as Facebook, Twitter, Skype, BlackBerry chat, 2go, WhatsApp, Badoo, Instagram, UberSocial, YouTube, videogames, and the like. They perform poorly academically when compared with those who spend less time on these distracting activities. The more movies viewed and the more social networking sites visited, the less time is available to be focused on studying and completing assignments. The problem is not just visiting these sites, but also time spent in it as well as the effects on one's sub-consciousness. Some students are so addicted to these sites that they browse even while the lecture is going on as depicted below.

OTHER INDIVIDUAL-RELATED OBSTACLES

Tell me, how these students could benefit from the lecture? Of course they are physically present in the classroom, but obviously absent-minded. Some students even engage in Facebook and BlackBerry chats while their books are opened before them in the library. It is that bad! If you really want to help yourself, my advice is that you drastically limit the time you allot to those distractions. You should explore more of the aspect of those modern technologies that are relevant and more useful to your today's business that is academics.

You might emulate the Irish novelist Maria Edgeworth by saying '*All work and no play makes Jack a dull boy*', but remember to complete the saying '*All play and no work makes Jack a mere toy*'. You can do these things only when you have justified your day academically. I keep emphasizing academic work because academic excellence is the subject of the discourse here. So long as you remain a regular student, your business is nothing else but your studies. Nothing should compete with the time you spend studying daily, nothing whatsoever. You will be solely responsible for your poor performance if you forget this simple fact. You often blame the Nigerian educational system without doing your own part. Your poor performance will become exaggerated in such excellent educational institutions as University of Yale, Harvard University, Cambridge University, Massachusetts Institute of Technology, University of Oxford, University of London and the like if you cannot pay maximum attention to your studies.

THE LADDER TO ACADEMIC EXCELLENCE

Have you ever bothered to find out the underlying reasoning for manufacturing phones with very sophisticated features? Is it to limit or enhance your productiveness? My dear, it is to enable you achieve more. For instance, you can access the dictionary anywhere with your phone without waiting to get home to consult for new words. But the question now is, what is the size of your vocabulary? The web browser on your phone is for you to keep abreast with developments across the globe. How often do you use it for this purpose? What is the essence of you carrying a BlackBerry phone, iPad, Android, iPhone, and wireless-enabled phones if you are no better than someone using a Nokia 3310 phone? What is the justification for you having a computer laptop that you use only for watching movies and playing music? What use are textbooks when you only use them to decorate your book rack or table in school or at home? Instead of wasting your time engaging in a long telephone discussion or telephone chat while travelling, why not pick up a book and read along? Remember the danger of sticking the phone to your ear for a long time, think about the effect of the radiation. It may have the capacity to damage your hearing.

Your phone browser or laptop is there to help you improve yourself academically and not diminish your productiveness. Limit the number of hours you spend in these activities and divert more time to your study and watch out for great improvement. Did I hear you say that you do these things but you still pass? I tell you if you pass while doing all those, you can do better if you spend less time on them. By the way, what category of pass do you mean? The simple truth is that whatever level, if you allocate more time to your studies, your grades will certainly change for the better. If your average grade was C, then you have potentials for grade B and so on. Even if your current average grade is A, why not aim at being the overall best? Try it, I am sure you will send me a mail testifying. If you have a laptop or a phone that can browse, challenge yourself by keeping abreast of national and global news. You should be greatly informed about many things in your field and other fields. You are meant to educate others who do not have access to these things. The internet and the phone facilities are for your improvement not deterioration!

Dealing with Your Addiction

You already know that too much television viewing can steal your time and productivity. You do not necessarily have to stop watching television in order to achieve your academic goals, but watching during your peak performance time can hinder your progress. *Watch your favourite movies and get on the social sites only when you have justified your day academically.* Do these during your non-critical periods and then only for a reasonably short period, because if you do it far into the night, it will render you weak and exhausted the next day. Use all the new technology to your benefit and do not ever allow television, laptop, iPad, Android, and BlackBerry to steal the precious hours you have available during the day.

Bad Sleeping Habits

Most students oftentimes have the habit of staying up late to watch movies, gossip, hang out, chat, go to nightclubs, make free midnight calls. These things make them tired and very exhausted the next day. Lack of sufficient sleep does affect the functioning of the brain and the entire human body network. You find yourself sleeping when you should be in class or sleeping on your books in the library or classroom as shown in the picture. You sleep even while the teacher is teaching in the class. Students are encouraged to get at least six hours of sleep every night. Of course, you can get your six hours' sleep comfortably and still keep your academic flag flying. *It only requires proper time management.* I learnt from Prof C. C. Soludo, former governor of Central Bank of Nigeria, who himself is a first-class graduate and best graduating student in all his academic programmes (BSc—PHD) from the University of Nigeria, Nsukka, that immediately after class while in school, he would take his siesta after which he would go to prefab and read till midnight at least. That means eight hours at a stretch! And I bet you are aware of his achievements across the globe. For this world-acclaimed icon, it is very important to study sufficiently and also get enough sleep by appropriate management of your time. So how about you? Do you study enough and at the same time sleep enough?

Not Exercising

Another problem you might have as a student is not making out time for exercise. Or are you? Are you in the league of those that see exercising as the business of the obese? Is the lady exercising in the picture above obese? Non-regular exercise keeps you dull and heavy, even in your brain. It makes you lazy. On the other hand, exercise keeps one physically fit and mentally alert! Regular exercise is needed to keep one physically healthy, but more importantly, it is needed for cognitive functioning. Exercise increases blood flow to the hippocampus in the brain, and this part of the brain is important for learning and memory. It also reduces the stress levels. It is advisable that a student engages in at least fifteen minutes of exercise each day. Most renowned achievers I know or read about never joke with their daily exercise.

Bad Eating Habits

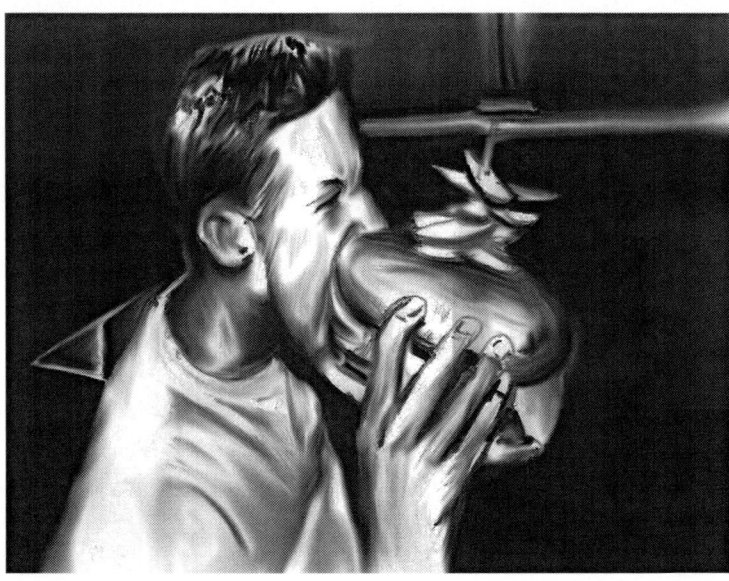

Due to a hectic school schedule, you may be tempted to skip breakfast, and sometimes lunch, to quickly go through your daily activities. You may not only skip meals, but may be more inclined to eating fast foods that are high in fat and cholesterol and low in calories. These meals do not provide sufficient nutrients for your body and energy that is needed for you to efficiently go through the day. A diet high in cholesterol and saturated fat is also known to have *a detrimental effect on cognitive functioning*.[93] When you go shopping for foodstuff, you should purchase more fruits and vegetables that take little time to prepare. Purchase foods that are high in omega-3 fatty acids, such as sardines, cooked soybeans, walnut, cabbage, etc. They improve *learning and memory*. As much as possible, reduce intake of fast food, food with artificial colouring and sodas. It is advisable to take them only occasionally.

Learning from Bad Experience

You can learn from your past. This should motivate you to modify your approach and achieve a better result in the future. First you must think of how a bad experience can be a motivator. For instance, a lot of students complain that they read well but obtained discouraging results and so decide that it is not worthwhile reading anymore. If this happens to you, that may be a signal that there is something you are not doing right. It is either that your approach to answering the questions is not right or that the points made were sketchy. While I was an undergraduate, I made 68 (B grade; A grade starts from 70) in seven of my courses. I felt bad because I expected to make As in those courses. But I was not deterred though I felt very bad at first. I felt that I could have worked less and settled for 60 instead (since B = 60-69). But I later said to myself that was not an acceptable excuse to work Less just as Rudyard Kipling said '*We have forty million reasons for failure, but not a single excuse.*'[94] Then I figured out what the real truth might be. Maybe I was feeling I had written enough, maybe there were points I left out. Since then, I worked better and made better grades. I decided that in my examinations, I would write exhaustively from texts, notes, examples, and personal understanding, and it helped me a lot. That idea worked! So your failure should motivate you to work harder, not dissuade you. Listen to Dale Carnegie: '*Develop success from failures. Discouragement and failure are two of the surest stepping stones to success*',[95]

The next step is to continue focusing on what you want to achieve. Use that to motivate yourself to try again. There is no need to get frustrated or disappointed. This will only set you back. If you feel *frustrated*, feel it in a positive way. Because when you are frustrated, it means that you are about to have a *breakthrough*! Just pause and ask yourself some questions. Examine yourself and watch out for such habits or attitudes in you (see box). If they are

Habits That Destroy Your Academic Future

- Lack of ambition
- Truancy
- Lateness to lectures
- Absenteeism
- Poor relationship with teachers due to bad attitude
- Nonchalant attitude towards assignments and even tests and exams
- Examination anxiety
- Indiscipline
- Cramming / rote learning / memorization
- Overconfidence

there, then something is wrong and you should fix it. A very powerful enemy is threatening your future and that enemy is *you*. You have yourself to blame if you submit yourself to this enemy. If you are already a victim in this kind of condition, you still have a chance to free yourself, but you must take a very bold step now. If not, the situation may keep worsening until you slip into a more dangerous level where your anxiety and depression will have deepened beyond remedy.

Take steps to handle these personal conditions, anxiety, and depression so as to repair your emotional status as regards to your academic life. These are natural effects of academic failure that keep building up with time. You need to know about such conditions and how to manage them.

CHAPTER TWELVE

Other External Factors, Problems, Obstacles and Their General Effects

A failure establishes only this, that our determination to succeed was not strong enough.[96]

—Christian Nestell Boveen (1820-1904), American writer

Though this book largely focuses on the student factor as contributory to academic failure, it is pertinent to equally recognize that other factors, apart from the student factor, are equally contributory. There are some other stakeholders whose actions and or inactions constitute part or cause of the problem. Some of these stakeholders are the government, education authorities, the teachers, education policymakers, lawmakers, administrators, parent, lecturers, et al. The actions or inactions of these institutions and stakeholders conduce to create disorder and undermine the goals of education (Neff, Hsich and Deitterat, 2005). The problems and challenges emanating from these stakeholders being largely exogenous are beyond the direct control of the students, yet they affect the students' academic work and performance in no small measure.

The Government

No doubt, Nigeria's education system in the twenty-first century faces a myriad of challenges. The long-standing ones include those of finance and funding, the growth of private higher education institutions, academic freedom, quality and excellence, governance and autonomy, efficiency, and management challenges.[97] Others are gender equality, research and publishing and the problems of scholarly communication, language issues, and the migration of talent or brain drain. These are but a few of the problems that have laid the higher education sector prostrate. Now, these old challenges have been augmented by new challenges linked to the growing role of knowledge in economic development, rapid changes in telecommunications technology, and the globalization of trade and labour markets (Salmi, 2001).

In Nigeria, it is the norm to heap the blame for the falling standard of education in Nigeria on governments. Indeed, the government has critical role to play, particularly in the provision of the infrastructure necessary to create conducive atmosphere for academic and scholarly pursuits through adequate funding. However, as we can see for the challenges enumerated above, the challenge of funding is only one of the contributory factors to the decline of education in Nigeria, albeit an important one. Unfortunately, time and space would not permit me to exhaustively discuss these challenges in detail. From my little research, it would appear that the federal government has been making some remarkable improvements in its funding of the education sector in the recent past.

The present administration of President Goodluck Jonathan is making moves to grant autonomy (for them to start generating their funds internally, not solely depending on government subvention) to the nation's foremost universities—University if Ibadan, University of Lagos, University of Nigeria, University of Benin, Ahmadu Bello University, and Obafemi Awolowo University. The government set up Mr Steve Orosanye to lead the committee on financial autonomy. This committee noted that the Nigeria's tertiary standard has been declining in the past twenty-five years, with the best of the nation's universities not ranking among the world's best 6,000.

It may also interest you to know that President Goodluck Ebele Jonathan's administration through the Tertiary Education Trust Fund (TETFund), formerly known as Education Trust Fund (ETF), now concentrates on intervention in tertiary institutions. There is a progressive upgrading of the facilities in the institutions to enhance teaching and learning. TETFund high-impact fund aims to nurture institutions across the geopolitical zones to make them emerge as centres of excellence. According to the information from federal ministry of education, ministerial platform on key achievements in commemoration of the first anniversary of President Goodluck Ebele Jonathan's administration, a paper presented by the then Hon Minister of Education Prof Ruqayyatu Ahmed Rufai'I, the improvement in funding is in the third phase now as follows: Under the first phase (2009), six including the Universities of Ibadan, Benin, Ilorin, Maiduguri, ABU, and UNN each received N3 billion. Under the same phase, Yabatech, Kaduna, and Akanu Ibiam polytechnics each received N1 billion. Three Colleges of Education, namely Kotangora, Gombe, and Omoku, also received N1 billion each. During the second phase (2010), the Universities of Jos, Port-Harcourt, Bayero-Kano, Abubarka Tafawa Balewa-Bauchi, Federal University of Technology, Owerri and Obafemi Awolowo University, Ile-Ife, each received N3 billion. The three polytechnics of Lokoja, Mubi, and Institute of Management and Technology, Enugu, each received N1 billion. The Colleges of Education at Gumel, Afaha-Nsit, and Adeyemi were not left at this stage as they received N1 billion each. The Usman Dan Fodio Universities, Sokoto, and National Defense University each received N3 billion under the third phase (2011). Under this phase, Benue State Polytechnic, Ugbokolo, and Abia State each received N1 billion, so did the Colleges of Education at Yobe State, Gashua, and FCE Abeokuta.

In general, the federal government of Nigeria has progressively increased investment in education from N234.8 billion in 2010, as N356.4 billion in 2011 to N409.5 billion in 2012.[98] Education has the highest budgetary allocation of N426.53 billion in the 2013 budgetary proposals. Government has also been supplying secondary schools with the necessary equipments for subjects like home management. I was quite impressed to witness the delivery of these materials to two different government secondary schools in Jikwoyi, a suburb of Abuja, the nation's capital.

From the above developments, it is obvious that the government has been improving on its funding of education. Despite these improvements, however, the truth remains that government cannot read for the student. Students need do their own share for the full impact of the government's effort to have the desired effect.

My advice to the students is, therefore, to do their part and tidy up their end first. Do not allow the poor infrastructure and dysfunctional educational policies overwhelm you. For instance, labour-related strike frequently embarked upon by academic staff of higher institutions has had the undesired effect of disrupting the academic calendar, frustrating students and parents alike. It has largely been responsible for the sharp rise in students' enrolment into institutions outside Nigeria. According to Vanguard newspaper of 7 June 2012, over 71,000 Nigerian students pay N160 billion tuition fees (40 per cent of the 2012 education budget in Ghana).[99] Nigerians studying in British and American universities have spent over N137,023 billion on tuition and living expenses in the last two academic sessions, about 34 per cent when measured against the federal government's allocation to education.

My take on the situation is that students have a number of self-help measures that can help blunt the unsavoury effects of exogenous factors. For instance, knowing that the strike will eventually be called off, the student should use the period of the strike to make up for work not adequately covered during the session, make up for areas of deficiency, and the like. Students should regard strike periods as 'bonus' time provided to catch up with academic work. There is also the often talked about sexual abuse in higher institutions. At times, the student themselves are instrumental in creating the environment for their abuse. Where a student spends all her time in watching movies, attending clubs, and engaging in all manners of extracurricular activities, there is a very big possibility that they would end up with poor grades. This opens them up for abuse. My question is, are you sure you are not facilitating your abuse? Is that skimpy skirt not designed primarily to attract the opposite sex, students and lecturers alike? The key is, in every situation, try and play your part as a student well first.

The University of Ilorin student's guide summarizes the main causes of academic failure to include the following:

- Negative attitude to education
- Lack of goal/ambition
- Truancy
- Absenteeism
- Playfulness
- Poor study habits
- Inattentiveness
- Lateness to lectures/classes
- Waste of time and energy on activities that are not academically oriented (e.g., watching television/video and attending parties)
- Lack of cordiality with teachers
- Non-reading of relevant textbooks
- Negative influence of bad friends

- Poor memory
- Overconfidence
- Ill health
- Negative attitude to homework/assignments
- Poor attitude to test / examination anxiety
- Indiscipline (e.g., reliance on examination malpractice and drug abuse)
- Procrastination
- Memorization/cramming/rote learning
- Poor self-concept

They result in academic failure, affective reaction, anxiety, and depression.

The first consequence of truancy in the academic environment is *failure*. At the institutional level, academic problems among students can create disorder and undermine the general mission of schools (Neff, Hsieh and Dejitterat, 2005). Students usually attribute academic failure to such factors as difficulty of questions, lack of studying facilities, wrong timing and schedule of examinations as in a case where a student writes different examination almost at the same time. This usually happens to students referring some courses or, in cases of electives, poor quality of teachers (the kind of teachers that will not teach what they ought to but set questions that many students find difficult to cope with), marking methodology, peer influences, poor study habits, low level of preparations, low ability, and too much social outings.

As regards to *affective reactions*, the way and manner individuals react to success or failure in examinations differ. Some people receive the results of examinations with pent-up fear of failure and be overcome with emotions when the outcome is below expectation. Others have a nonchalant attitude towards the outcome of examinations. Affective reactions often depend on how the outcome is achieved. Outcomes achieved through action generally lead to more intense affective reactions than the same outcomes achieved through inaction (Crosnoe, 2002). This suggests that when students work hard to achieve success in an examination, their affective reaction is more intense than when they did not take concrete actions to achieve success. High achievers in examinations often attribute the causes of their success to effort, ability, intelligence, and emotional stability, while low achievers attribute causes of failure to ability and difficult examination (Le Foll and Rascle, 2006).

Obstacles such as poor quality of teachers, marking methodology, peer influences, poor study habits, low level of preparations, and the like affect students by raising the levels of *anxiety*. Chronic anxiety is symptomatic of an underlying problem. This anxiety results in restlessness, irritability, insomnia, lack of interest and withdrawal from usual activities, frequent crying, poor school performance, and truancy. Playing your part well and taking your academic work seriously will certainly reduce your level of anxiety and produce better results.

Another major effect of academic failure is *depression*—a state of unhappiness and hopelessness. This is a psychiatric disorder in which a person exhibits such symptoms as persistent feelings of hopelessness, dejection, poor concentration, lack of energy, inability to sleep, and sometimes suicidal tendencies (Encarta Dictionary, 2009). Many students, in the event of failure, feel bad, feel like leaving school, feel inferior to others, hate themselves, feel emotionally disturbed (see picture above). A few, though, feel there is always another chance and try to maintain their normal selves, while many feel like giving up. This generally shows that majority of students do not feel pleased with failure. I am yet to see a student who is happy after failing an examination. But like the saying goes, *had I known*

always comes last. Unfortunately, you cannot turn back the hands of time to do it better. The best way to handle this kind of situation is to take failure as a challenge.

Failure, according to Henry Ford (1863-1947), the founder of the Ford Motor Company, should be seen as *'the opportunity to begin again more intelligently'*.[100] I therefore urge you to take it as a challenge. Prepare not to let it happen again. Be positive in your thinking. Make positive pronouncements. Say 'I will never fail again.' 'I must attain academic excellence.' Think and affirm along such lines. You also need to commit your resolve to God in prayer and be honest to yourself. However, please do remember that hard work and doing the right thing at the right place at the right time is the greatest prayer. You have to believe that you can make the difference in your situation.

Napoleon Hill said that *'the man who wins . . . is the man who thinks he can win'*.[101] You just need to review your methods and attitude. Redefine your goals, chart a new path, and work harder. Do not even think of giving up because that is not an option. That will be making the worst mistake that you will live to regret your entire life. But if you have not had such experience yet, you need not wait. It is better to work now than wait to experience failure. If at first you do not succeed, find out why before you try again, maybe there was something you did not do right!

"My experience has thought me that a man is ever quite near success as when that which he calls failure has overtaken him, he thinks accurately and with persistency he discovers that so called failure is usually nothing more than a signal to rearm himself with a new plan or purpose."[102]

SECTION THREE

Determination

CHAPTER THIRTEEN

How Determined Are You?

There is no chance, no destiny, no fate, can circumvent or hinder or control the firm resolve of a determined soul. Gifts count for nothing; will alone is great; all things give way before it soon or late. What obstacle can stay the mighty force of the sea-seeking river in its course, or cause the ascending orb of the day to wait? Each well-born soul must win what it deserves. Let the fool prate of luck. The fortunate is he whose earnest purpose never swerves, whose slightest action or inaction serves the one great aim.[103]

Ella Wheeler Wilcox (1850-1919),
American author and poet

Determination is the willpower needed for action. It is a matter of the made-up mind, firmness of purpose, and firm commitment to a course of action. It was Denis Waitley, an American motivational speaker and bestselling author, who said, *'Determination gives you the resolve to keep going in spite of the roadblocks that lay before you.'* [104] William Mathews supported this view when he said, *'Of all the elements of success, none is more vital than self-reliance—a determination to be one's own helper and not to look for others for support. It is the secret of all individual growth and vigour, the master key that unlocks all difficulties in every profession or calling.'* [105]

Determination is one of the keys to success. Oftentimes, people know exactly what they need to do in order to achieve the level of success they want in their academic work, but are still not able to make it happen. One big reason is that they give up too early and easily. No one ever said reaching your dreams is going to be so easy; after all, nothing good really comes easy. When you want to achieve the best, you need to be the best too.

Higher-quality good requires a higher price too. Pay the price now to enjoy a higher quality of life tomorrow.

In truth, there are only very few people at the top of the ladder of excellence anywhere in the world. This is because most of us are too weak to break out from the crowd at the bottom of the ladder. With strong determination and perseverance, you have no boundaries or obstacles that are insurmountable. Determination to succeed is the only thing that can put your name in the pages of history, the Yellow Pages, or Guinness World Records. Without determination, my dear, your goal will forever remain just a goal—a mere dream.

Thomas Fuller (1608-1661), an English churchman and historian, affirmed this when he said, *'An invincible determination can accomplish almost anything and in this lies the great distinction between great men and little me (men).'* [106]

It is true that no one can go back and make a brand-new start, but anyone can start from now and make a brand-new ending! 'Four short words sum up what has lifted most successful individuals above the crowd: *a little bit more*. They did all that was expected of them and a little bit more,'[107] says A. Lou Vickery, an American business author. The difference between you and those adjudged as 'gurus' in your class is that they read their books *a little bit more* than you; they listen to lectures/their teachers with *a little bit more* concentration than you did; they answer their examination questions with *a little bit more* conviction and explanations than you did; they make their points *a little bit more* logical than you do; they pursue their academic goals with *a little bit more* determination than you did; they are *a little bit more* focused than you; they do their assignment with *a little bit more* research and dedication than you did; they give their studies *a little bit more* time than you do. On your part, you entertain distractions like phone chats, frequenting nightclubs, showing off, procrastination, fear, and the like *a little bit more* than they did. Check it out. If this is it true for you, then you need, according to Brian Tracy, to develop the winning edge; small differences in your performance can lead to large differences in your results.

You do not lack the strength to pursue your academic goal. What I think you may lack is the will and it is paramount that you fortify your will as this is the distinguishing factor between those scoring straight As and those wallowing in Es and referrals. Vincent T. Lombardi (1913-1970), an

American football coach, made this clear in his statement, '*The difference between a successful person and others is not a lack of strength, not a lack of knowledge, but rather a lack of will.*'[108] When you are determined to vigorously pursue your dream, you will surely make something great out of it. '*Continuous, unflagging effort, persistence and determination will win. Let not the man be discouraged who has these,*'[109] says James Whitecomb Riley.

A goal without determination to pursue it is like a car without an engine. It cannot move! Heed Paul J. Meyer supports this when he said, '*Crystallize your goals. Make a plan for achieving them and set yourself a deadline. Then with supreme confidence, determination and disregard for obstacles and other people's criticisms carry out your plan.*' [110] Without determination, you end up achieving nothing despite your beautiful array of aspirations. This was confirmed by Napoleon Bonaparte when he said, '*The truest wisdom is a resolute determination. When my resolution is taken all is forgotten except what will make it succeed.*' [111] Also Confucius (551-479 BCE), a Chinese teacher, editor, politician, and philosopher of the spring and autumn of Chinese history, supported that with his remark that '*the general of a large army can be defeated, but you cannot defeat a determined mind*'.[112] You need to be determined to achieve something great. Be determined to pursue your goal with much vigour. Do not just settle for *good* when *better* is possible. Do not limit yourself. Art Sepulveda advised, '*Be a history maker and a world shaker.*'[113] Tell yourself that it is possible, that you can do it; you can even exceed that benchmark. Set a high target and charge after it with so much determination.

Everything is possible. Do not ever use the phrase 'never possible'. Like Oscar Wilde, an Irish writer and poet (1854-1900), said, '*Moderation is a fatal thing and nothing succeeds like excess.*' [114] If you devalue your dreams, no one else will raise the price. Great leaders and achievers never settle for other people's standard because they are determined to pursue what many regard as impossible. Tell me, who said that you are too inferior to make excellent grades in school? All you need to do is to clearly define the result you intend to achieve as this will help in sustaining your determination. Determination is simply the willpower to achieve. It does not need to be super or extraordinary. It simply requires more persistence and consistency.

CHAPTER FOURTEEN

Motivation for Determination

Life takes on meaning when you become motivated, set goals and charge after them in an unstoppable manner.[115]

—Les Brown (1912-2001), motivational speaker

I need to ask you this question, why do you want to be successful in your academic work and in your other life pursuits? Is it to be a model, to break records in your field, and be popular in the world? Do you want to be a renowned scholar, to have your name engraved in the sands of time, to make positive headlines nationally and across the globe, to be a trendsetter, to be respected by both the young and the old because of your intellectual prowess, or is it just to make money or make a living? Is it merely to follow the crowd? The list continues. Are you sure about your answer? If not, you really need to *pause now* and *reflect on* the reason you want to be successful.

If you have done that, then that reason should be and is your *motivating factor*! Determination can be likened to a car, while motivation is like the fuel that makes movement possible. These two cannot simply work without the other. They complement each other. You cannot be motivated without the determination to act. *'Motivation alone is not enough. If you have an idiot and you motivate him, now you have a motivated idiot,'*[116] says Jim Rohn.

In the academic sense, *learning* is only possible when there is *motivation*. Motivation can be seen as the element that initiates and sustains a person's own involvement in learning. If a student is strongly motivated, he puts in all his or her effort, personality, time, energy, and financial resources into achieving his or her set goal, which in this case is academic excellence. Your academic life can take a better turn when you have motivation.

I acknowledge the fact that different people have different motivating factors. What motivates person A may not motivate person B. Many students are motivated but do not know how to use it. It is paramount to understand that positive motivation is very essential in achieving success in whatever one is doing in life. It is a necessary and sufficient condition for success because it acts as a propelling force towards the attainment of success. Without positive motivation, there will be no positive action.

The question to you right now is, are you motivated at all? If yes, is it positive or negative? I want you to understand that the first step to attaining academic excellence and success in every other life endeavour is self-motivation. Second, the motivation must be positive and consistent. That means you must stay motivated always, else you are bound to derail along. The force must remain permanent and intensive.

In line with Patrick Chan's e-book, *'Motivation is influenced by two powerful factors . . . It's either Pain or Pleasure.'* This simply means that your motivation is either to avoid pain—in this context, *academic failure*—or to achieve pleasure—*academic excellence*. Most times, trying to avoid the pain of academic failure seems to be the stronger motivating factor. You do not want to imagine yourself being unhappy, feeling you have lost, feeling that everybody will see you as the dullest in your class; your parents, relations, and friends will not be proud of you but disappointed. So to avoid feeling downcast, dejected, rejected, and inferior, you are motivated to pursue excellence to the best of your ability. When you view pain this way, you will see that it is like a friend that encourages you to take the *bull by the horn* in the bid to achieve your goal—academic excellence!

The question to you, the reader, now is, are you performing at your *summum puntum* (optimal point)? If the answer is yes, bravo; but if not, *why not?* When one is motivated, one takes the complementary action to achieve one's target.

I will adapt the following mathematical representation: **Motivation + Action = Results = Success (MARS)**.

In this context, I can say that motivation is the energy to study, to achieve, and to maintain these positive behaviours over time. I must tell you that it is not very easy to have and sustain motivation. You really need to constantly work to increase, improve, support, sustain, or strengthen your motivation through a number of useful tips:

- **Personal conviction that success fosters success**. When you get into the success loop, everything about you keeps keying into more success. It is true that everybody wants to be successful, but the only people who end up being successful are the ones who are willing to do the hard work today to have a successful start. Remember that *the only place where success comes before work is in the dictionary*. Nothing good comes easy after all! So whenever you feel the work is becoming too difficult or the target is becoming too demanding to achieve, just remind yourself that your success today will help you in becoming even more successful tomorrow. Studying is like putting credit into your bank account. Every effort counts. Keep the end goal in view! That end goal is the motivator.
- **Personal conviction that your education is the foundation for your success in the future**. Just like the knowledge learned in the first year forms the foundation to subsequent courses at a higher level, success achieved in school will serve as a foundation for future life successes. With a good academic background, your potential for success is much enhanced in your future endeavours. You need to, according to Stephen Covey, the author of *The 8th Habit: From Effectiveness to Greatness*, 'Begin with the end in mind.'[117]
- **See academic success as the only route to this successful future**. This means that learning must be your number one priority at this time. Although socializing and recreational activities are important and are not to be totally ignored, but they must take a backseat in your academic programming.
- **Set out realistic goals to help you get there**. Try setting goals during a specific timelines of a day, week, month, or semester. The different courses actually require different approaches and different levels of attention. For instance, in economics, you find that such courses as econometrics, operations research, public finance, macroeconomics, microeconomics, and the like really require more time and attention than some other courses. The situation is the same in all other disciplines. So that means you need to give more attention to such courses. Reduce the task into smaller parts. That way, it will be easier for you to monitor and evaluate your progress and you will certainly be better motivated to continue.

- **Set performance target for yourself and learn how to work harder when you underperform.** Highly motivated students operate at a very high frequency. They view their effort and ability as the most important factors of their success. In cases where they fail to achieve their target, they work harder to fill the gap.
- **You need to always compete with yourself.** Keep improving on your previous grades rather than focusing on the performance of others. Focus on the number of A grade you scored in the last semester and the number you intend to add in the next semester.
- **Remember the five Ps, that is; proper preparation prevents poor performance.**

This chapter can be summarized in Patrick Chan's words as follows:

It is the ACTION that you take that makes you become successful . . . that is why I say that motivation is the key for you to be successful. Without motivation, there will not be action from you. And without action, there will not be results!!! The results you want in life are linked directly to the motivation you have. If you can imagine your own success, you will be motivated to take action towards it. So, with the actions you take, you will get the results to achieve the success that you want.[118]

So what are you still waiting for? Get up and define your goal that will serve as your motivation! Then, maintain your momentum up the ladder!

Remember the words of Mahatma Gandhi that "*Strength does not come from physical capacity. It comes from an indomitable will*"[119] Brian Tracy advised, '*Resolve to pay any price or make any sacrifice to get to the top 10 percent in your field. The payoff is incredible.*'[120]

SECTION FOUR

Efforts

CHAPTER FIFTEEN

Eliminate Fear and Limiting Belief

Life put together is made up of 10% of what happens to you and 90% of your reaction to what has happened to you.[121]

—John Spence

The big fish is not caught in shallow waters. You have to go into the open sea.[122]

—Tai Solarin (1922-1994), one of Nigeria's foremost educationists and social activists

The previous chapters explained in detail the first three parts of this book, namely, *focus*, *ideas*, and *determination*. This and the next few chapters dwell exclusively on *effort*. I want you to understand the fact that success is sweet, but its secret is sweat. To achieve success, there must be aspiration, inspiration, and perspiration. That is where effort comes in. Colin Powel, an American statesman and a retired four star general said *"A dream doesn't become reality through magic. It takes sweat, determination and hard work."*[123]

Every outstanding success is built on the ability to do better than good enough! The hardest thing about climbing the ladder of success is getting through the crowd at the bottom. For you to really avoid academic failure, therefore, it is important you deal with these identified obstacles. Dealing with these obstacles successfully requires you to set achievable but not mediocre goals at the beginning of the school year and at the beginning of each semester. Be determined to make it and work hard to achieve the set goals.

Identify and Fight Your Fear

Believe it or not, FEAR is the one thing that can stifle academic performance. It is mostly termed 'anxiety', and as a student, you experience it during tests, when you are tensed, stressed, or simply when you are unprepared. Despite setting goals and studying, FEAR can completely erode your efforts. It can make you lose focus and think that you will fail and not reach your goals. Always remember this: FEAR is False Evidence Appearing Real—FEAR is not real. Whenever you experience anxiety or fear, remember you do not have to, because failure is only a fake appearance of reality, it is not real.

So in school and in life, never entertain FEAR! All you need to do is to get rational about your fears. By this I mean that you should identify the primary cause or source of your fear. Fear of the unknown is always the strongest. Fear can be used as a good motivator. Get to identify your fears and act on them—do not react to them. Fear is a secondary emotion. The key is to identify the primary cause or source, think about it and act on it. The causes of behaviour are usually easier to address than the symptoms, like fear. Your greatest fear should be that of wasting a potentially defining moment because of fear.

Uncertainty

But there is another reason that weakens your motivation. That is *uncertainty*. When you feel uncertain, you will lose the drive. Have you ever been in any competition, especially sports? If you see your opponent as someone who is going to win, what will happen? You will feel uncertain about yourself, and the next thing you know, you are already not motivated to compete. You will feel very inferior. You will 'lose' before you begin to compete in your mind. You will suffer a poor result as you will be participating just for the sake of participation and not because you are motivated to achieve the results. There is a very big difference between doing something because you are really convinced and forcing yourself just to fulfil all righteousness. Make sure you are certain before you take action. You can be certain by using the *power of pain and pleasure* to motivate yourself correctly. That is why all motivated people are confident people as they are certain about what they are about to do. They are certain about what they want to achieve. They are confident in achieving the results they want from the action they will take. When your mind and actions are in alignment, your motivation will increase to achieve your results. This is the best way for you to get motivated instantly. It only takes a few minutes to exercise your thoughts to do this. It will motivate you to do it if you know how to use the power of your thoughts positively. You can make that wonderful grade this semester. You can line up As. Believe that and work towards it. 'Your belief determines your action and your action determines your results, but first you have to believe,'[124] says Mark Victor Hansen.

Break Your Limiting Beliefs

You may also be held down by your own limiting beliefs. A limiting belief is a false belief that a person acquires as a result of making an incorrect conclusion or deduction about something in life or from a life's experience. According to Steve Pavlina, *'Limiting beliefs can seriously hold us back in life. But most of the time such beliefs are invisible to us. They control some of our thoughts and behaviors behind the scenes, enough to curtail our results in some area of life.'*[125] For example, if you have the false belief that you are not good enough, you do not matter, you are not lovable, then you will avoid many growth and learning experiences because you have to be willing to fail in order to build new skills. My question then is, are limiting beliefs stopping you from taking action that can lead you to success today?

How To Deal With Limiting Beliefs

Here is your action plan. First, you must destroy the limiting beliefs you have right now. To do this, write down the goal you want to achieve. Then, write down all the limiting beliefs you have that are preventing you from achieving your goals.

Now that you have listed them, please literally delete them in your mind now one after the other. Take action, do it! See the results you get and work it out from there to impove.

But sometimes you cannot just destroy limiting beliefs because it is not easy to change a belief system that has been engrained in your life for years. Here is a way to destroy it. You can destroy your limiting belief by associating with positive references. Associating with positive references will anchor your motivation so that you can have more confidence to take action. When you have a wrong reference, you will not be motivated to take appropriate action because you can only see the negative potential. If you have this kind of negative reference and start to feel unmotivated, what you should do is STOP! Search for references that have been proven to work for whatever action you want to take, it can be your classmate who is doing well. He or she is not different—he has just one head, two hands, and every other body part like you do. He or she is really not better than you, so why not take that as a challenge? Use the positive references as your 'point of reference' to hold up your belief system so that you are convinced that whatever action you want to take is possible. Knowledge is not power, **knowledge + action = power**. But you need motivation to support action.

Some Limiting Beliefs That Could Prevent You From Achieving Academic Excellence
<ul><li>I am too young?</li><li>I am too old?</li><li>I am too poor?</li><li>I am too dull?</li><li>I have too many commitments?</li><li>I am too handsome?</li><li>I am too beautiful?</li><li>I am too ugly?</li><li>I have less ability?</li><li>I am not worth it?</li><li>I am the worst among my mates?</li><li>I am so disadvantaged?</li><li>I am hunted by some evil spirit or some enemies?</li><li>I am the worst illiterate on earth?</li><li>I do not deserve the pleasant outcome (success)?</li></ul>

So the equation above can now be revised to be **knowledge + (action + motivation) = power**.

Many peer groups can be a positive influence on their friends as well. It is thought that intelligent students help their peers improve their grades. A newsletter I got from professional speaker and bestselling author of many books, Brian Tracy, on 21 November 2011 on unlimited potential, reads as follows:

> You have within you right now everything you could ever need or want to be a great success in every area of your life. Whether you are aware of it or not, you have deep reserves of potentials and ability that if properly harnessed and channeled, will enable you to accomplish extraordinary things with your life. The only real limits on what you can be, have or do are self-imposed. They

do not exist outside of you. Once you make a clear, unequivocal decision to cast off all your mental limitations and throw yourself wholeheartedly into the accomplishment of a great goal, your unlimited success is virtually guaranteed . . . as long as you do not stop. The truth is you learn most of your important lessons in life from experience, by looking back at what happened to you, evaluate those experiences and ideally extract ideas and insights from them that you can then apply to the future.[126]

Example of this experience is either learning from your failure (that you did not read as you ought to have) or from your success (that you read more to achieve more success).

Eleanor Roosevelt (1884-1962), a social activist and a former American First Lady reminds you that "*The future belongs to those who believe in the beauty of their dreams*[127] while Walt Disney, an American film producer and philanthropist encourages you saying "*If you can dream it, you can do it . . .*"[128]

CHAPTER SIXTEEN

You Must Have Attitude

Attitudes alter abilities.[129]

—John Mason

'You have to put in many, many, many tiny efforts that nobody sees or appreciates before you achieve anything worthwhile,' [130] says Brian Tracy. There are some common but important academic friendly class attitudes you need to imbibe as a student. Listed below are main examples:

Result-Oriented Class Attitude

- Consistent attendance.
- Be prepared and on time.
- Pay attention.
- Take good notes; class notes are personal observations.
- The 84% of students who make an A or B attend class regularly.
- Front and middle seats tend to correlate with As and Bs.

Attend Your Lectures and On Time Too

Form the habit of being in class before the lecturer/teacher enters the class. Ensure that you always get a good position where you could hear what the teacher is saying and see what he is doing. When you get to class early, it gives you a little time to relax and calm your nerves after perhaps a walk from your hostel. This makes for better assimilation of the topic.

Pay Attention While the Class Is Going On

When in class, it is always advisable to pay attention to the teacher so as to capture everything he says, his explanations and examples. Watch out for the teacher's emphasis in class. Most times, that is what will give you an edge over other people in the examination. Even if the teacher dictates notes, sometimes he will pause to explain certain things that are not included in the note. A wise student will put down such explanations as part of his own note. Others might just be waiting for the teacher to continue with the note dictation. A minute's distraction in the class can make you miss something very important that might save you on the examination day. Also note that student participation in class increases learning. So be bold, have confidence, and feel free to ask questions in class.

Take Notes in Class

It is very necessary that a student attends classes and takes his notes by himself. Do not rely on notes from your classmate except if it is unavoidable. You will inadvertently be transferring another student's appreciation or misunderstanding of the topic to yourself. The person might not write some important things, maybe because the person knew it before then or the person did not deem it important. As earlier emphasized, it is very important to note the things that your teacher spends more time on. His emphasis on such things reveals their importance. In fact, taking notes is a necessary condition for your academic success, while reading and understanding it is a sufficient condition. Your notes should always be your companion and guide.

Pre- and Post-Class Review

Try and review your notes before the class. This will help you to remember everything that have so far been covered in that subject/course. It helps you in obtaining a better appreciation of the day's topic as the lecturer/teacher may oftentimes make reference to them. It also keeps you prepared in case of impromptu tests. Post-class review helps you to retain what you learnt that day without much stress and generally reduces the task of reading through lengthy notes before examinations. Reviewing your notes after class reduces your work preparatory to the examination to only a revision. Regular review also helps increase and reinforces your retention.

Good Time Management

The greatest feats in the world have been accomplished by those who systematized their work and organized their time. How do you spend your weekends, vacation, and time after classes? Make maximum use of every hour of your life. The future you hope to have is every minute drawing closer to you, so you need to prepare every minute to welcome it. Do not just lie on your bed in the hostel or stick out your head just watching, gossiping and criticizing the passers-by, their steps, dressing, or hairstyle. Proper use of your time in school differentiates you from the rest.

To actually achieve your goal, you must first know what needs to be done and when to do it.

- First, create a semester schedule and daily priority.
- Compare performance and adjust.
- Be efficient.
- Keep it simple.
- Schedule your time.

Has it occurred to you that you could be busy all day without achieving much? Setting priorities and effectively managing your time are vital in achieving your goals in life and getting to the top of the ladder of academic excellence. Here are some tips for effective scheduling and time management:

- Keep a long-term schedule (one year, four years, etc.) so that you can plan ahead and avoid missing important targets.
- Put all the major activities (tests, seminars, projects, etc.) into your calendar for the whole semester.
- Keep weekly and daily schedules. Plan ahead every week and every day. Create a to-do list daily.
- Review your learning style and take this into account when developing a study schedule.
- When setting up your schedule, utilize all sources of information available (course syllabus or scheme of work, term activities, calendar, class time table, etc.).

- Spread work out over the entire term, covering grounds steadily on day-to-day basis. Avoid few days rush and cramming or pulling an 'all-nighter' towards the examinations.
- When you memorize, you are as good as know next to nothing, because if you miss just a word in the sequence, you may completely go blank.

Study Time

To be academically successful, it is paramount to have a study schedule. To make a good study time table, you need to first of all determine your best study period. Is it early morning, night, or evening? Whichever time is best for you, you must use that time efficiently for optimal results. If you are not the night type, it means that making your reading schedule at night will be just a waste of time. You end up sleeping on your book. But remember that the greatest persons are people who toiled at night while their mates were asleep. That you are not a night reader does not mean you should not read. It takes self-discipline to do it, but it means that you will have to make maximum use of your day as well as early hours of the evening, preferably before midnight. Where you prefer to read in the evening, go to the library or select any other place that is conducive in the evening. Read from between, say, 4:30 p.m. and up till 9:30 p.m. It is also necessary you read in the morning before leaving for classes. You can comfortably read between 3:00 a.m. and 6:30 a.m. This way, you will get your normal six-hour sleep and at the same time put in quality time in your academic work. So what you need to do now is to *critique your study habits*.

For your private studies, please pay attention to the following key factors in your study habits:

- **Location**: Where should you study? The best study locations include a private, not-too-comfortable—to avoid napping—places, accessible to fresh air, secure, and with minimal distractions.
- **Time**: When and how much you study? When could be before and after class, find your high energy period—reading late into the night or waking early in the morning.
- **Method**: Check your study method. Do you read to understand, or you read to cram? The cramming syndrome is short-term, not practical, is academically unhealthy.

Form Study Groups

This practice helps a lot of students when they take it seriously. When I say study group, I mean reading partners, not gossip groups because some students use the opportunity of study groups only to bring each other up to date on the latest gossips.

In such a group, students must have a focus and a set of study priorities—address problem areas, ask questions, discuss areas the teachers/lecturers might emphasize in tests and examinations, solve past questions, and review questions in the textbooks.

Boost Your 'Sweet Spot'

A *sweet spot* in this context refers to that time of the day when you are likely to attain optimal concentration and achievement. It is paramount that you find out and know your own sweet spot by asking such questions as, What time do I perform optimally? What time can I read passionately and with great understanding and concentration?

For me, it is not every time of the day that I can read with optimal assimilation. So this is not what you jump into. That someone reads at a particular time does not mean you can also read with equal success at that time. It does not work that way. It is only at these *sweet spots* that you can achieve optimal results. Knowing your own *sweet spot* allows you to better design your reading plan. Match your *sweet spot* with your reading time. That way, you can predict your success and excellent performance. Give it a try! The most important thing you can do to achieve your goals is to make sure that as soon as you set them, you immediately begin to create momentum. '*The most important rules that I ever adopted to help me in achieving my goals were those I learned from a very successful man who taught me to first write down the goal, and then to never leave the site of my setting a goal without first taking some form of positive action toward its attainment. You see, in life, lots of people know what to do, but few people actually do what they know. Knowing is not enough! You must take action,*' warned Anthony Robbin.

CHAPTER SEVENTEEN

Study Attitude

I will study and prepare myself and someday I know my chance will come.[131]

—Abraham Lincoln (1809-1865), sixteenth president of the United States of America, serving from March 1861 until his assassination in April 1865

Study Sufficiently and Avoid Rushing

In the words of Albert Einstein, *'Never regard study as a duty but as an enviable opportunity to learn to know the liberating influence of beauty in the realm of the spirit for your own personal joy and to the profit of the community to which your latter work belongs.'*[132] To meet up with the demands of your academic works, you need to create a deadline for you to finish reading all your course materials for the first time. Also create sub-deadlines along the way for finishing particular chapters and topics.

STUDY ATTITUDE

Abigail Adams, the second first lady of the United States of America (1744-1818), remarked, *'Learning is not attained by chance; it must be sought for with ardour and attended to with diligence.'* [133] While making your study schedule, allot more time to the more difficult subjects/courses and make progress in the courses on an incremental basis, a little at a time. That is why it is good to start reading early so as to cover everything gradually and efficiently before your examination.

Always remember what Joseph Addison said, *'Reading is a basic tool in the living of a good life.'* [134] Reading only when the examinations are weeks away does not help at all. Instead it makes you clutter your brain with too much materials and information and consequently get confused in the examination hall. Even if you think you can cope with it, I tell you that you will be a lot better if you consider earlier preparation. Just give it a try and you will be convinced. It will not only make you better prepared with attendant bolstered confidence, but also make you prepare without much stress. You see? It's a lot better than doing the rush period thing.

If you feel overwhelmed, break down your task into smaller pieces, set goals for each segment, and achieve them one after the other until you cross the finish line. Studying, I must say, require your time and concentration, but I am sure it is worth the trouble. Think about the consequences of not studying. Weigh the consequences. What if I put this off? I might not finish this before the examination, then I will not get better passing grade or I might even fail this subject/course.

Effective Study

Sometimes you find yourself spending quite some time on a particular course/subject and still not understanding much. You should pause and ask yourself, 'Am I studying effectively?' In this case, you consider reviewing your study methods to see what you are not doing properly (Did you miss some major concepts?). You can also meet with your teacher, if not during consultation periods, then during classes as shown in the picture. Ten minutes spent getting help on a troublesome topic from the instructor may produce better results than a couple of hours on your own battling with it. Studying is a continuous process. A couple of days doing nothing may put you a lot farther behind than you think they will. Be steadfast! No vacillating!

Read the Textbook Effectively By Applying the SQ3R Method

S	Survey
Q	Question
R	Read
R	Recite
R	Review

How to Read the Textbook

'Reading is to the mind what exercise is to the body,' says Richard Steele, an Irish writer and politician (1962-1729).[135] You cannot study well without effective use of the textbook. Most textbooks are well-written and worthy of your careful reading. You should read the textbook several times in different ways to fully appreciate what it covers. Read before a lecture/class to see what is covered in the book and what you may need to pay special attention to during the lecture/class.

Read with the following questions in your mind: What is the topic of discuss? What does it mean? Can I picture or imagine it? What are the implications, merits and demerits? What is the latest thing I know about the topic? What problem are we trying to solve? What is the main theorem? How is it proved? What is the main formula? How is it derived? What are the main examples? How are they solved? Is there any relationship with the physical world? Can I think of any related example? If you do not understand the answers to these questions, then pay special attention during the lecture.

Read after classes to obtain a complete understanding of the material covered in the lecture. Did the instructor cover your questions? Are there parts of the topic you do not understand but you can study from the textbook? Read before tests to have a complete review. Read, think, and ask questions. Keep a balance of the three.

Tips for Effective Reading

- Scan through the chapter title(s).
- Look at pictures, graphs, figures, etc., and reading captions.
- Note underlined or italicized words or formulae.
- Read summary paragraphs or conclusions.
- Read the study questions at the end of chapters.
- Learn new reading techniques such as speed-reading, phrase-reading, survey-reading, etc.
- Write down key terms, phrases, and formulae.
- Go back and underline or highlight key sections and words.
- Answer study questions.
- Attempt sample problems.
- Get together with others in your class and ask each other questions on the readings.

- Make a simple outline of the material you read.
- Restate in your own words the essential definitions, ideas, formulas, and facts just read.
- Use multiple senses (hearing, seeing, speaking, writing, acting) that help in remembering.
- Review and re-read to increase comprehension and achievement.
- Formulate your own questions as you read.
- Periodic review will keep things fresh.

Summarize Each Chapter and the Course

You should have a summary for each chapter and a summary for the course at the end. Then it is much easier for you to understand and retrieve the material. Only well-organized knowledge can be remembered for a long time. Summarize the material for each topic. Once you have practiced and mastered the information in the chapter, you will have confidence that you have learned the topic. Now is the time to summarize. Remember that your goal of effective studying can be achieved by the following points: Set up goals, time management, preview, attend lectures and take notes, review and summarize, get the key facts, prepare and get the points.

> **Handling Study Challenges**
> - Engaging in a study group where your problems can be solved twice or thrice weekly.
> - Giving more attention to courses in which you are weak than others, e.g., engage in private reading and attend tutorial classes if any.
> - Studying with past question papers to enable you do adequate practice.
> - Being friendly with your course lecturers so that you will be free to seek assistance and ask questions from them.
> - Visiting the school library to read more on your area of specialization.
> - Asking questions on issues that are not clear and not pretending to know what you do not know.
> - Being active in class and showing zeal and interest.
> - Not abandoning each course for too long a time to avoid loss of interest.
> - Being computer literate in order to improve your research skills.

Dealing With Difficult Courses

Many students find some courses/subjects difficult to understand no matter how well lecturers/teachers try to explain. This may be due to poor study skills, negative attitude towards subjects/courses, lack of interest, negative influence of friends, absenteeism, etc.

Solving Problems and Dealing With Assignment

Schedule in advance to work on your assignments. When doing homework, you are actively applying your knowledge in solving problems. Reading textbook and attending classes are somewhat 'passive'. You get a much-better and deeper understanding and appreciation after solving some problems. In some sense, the more problems you solve, the deeper your appreciation of a topic, especially the more difficult ones. A grave mistake many students make is after arriving at the solution once, they assume they have mastered the problem. When such appears in the examination, students are unable to respond fast with a solution because they had not practiced enough. You need to practice to commit the solution to long-term memory. It is extremely important that you solve enough problems after your reading, lecture, and review. Getting the answers right is not your only goal (we already know the answer). It is the path you took in arriving at the answers that is important. It is only after you have applied the theorems and formulae many times can you achieve mastery of them. Then you can really say 'I got it'.

The most important secret to being a good problem solver is simply paying attention to the techniques, methods, or 'tricks' found from examples, proofs, and some of the problems. You should study each method thoroughly and know when and where to apply them. Normally, each chapter has several typical problems. A problem becomes 'typical' either because of its relation to a theorem, a formula, an application, or because of the solution method. You should be able to recognize the problems, make a thorough study of them, and know their possible variations. Always try to learn something unique from each problem you solved. After you are through with your homework, you should reflect on them again briefly to see what you have learned and what methods are worthy of keeping. This step is important for you to retain what you learned. Without this step, most of the effort you made doing the homework will simply be wasted.

Improving Your Memory

Sometimes you hear students complain that they went blank in the examination hall and could not remember what they learned. It happens a lot of times. Sometimes the student may remember those things after the examination and that makes you wonder why. If you think that you have strong retentive memory, but cannot keep and retrieve what you have learned, it does not make sense. One major reason for this type of forgetfulness is rushed reading, that is cramming too much information into the brain when examination is around the corner. This way, you overstretch your brain that it starts skipping some points when you need to recall the things you stored. But when you record things in your brain methodically by preparing early and gradually, recollection is a lot easier. It just flows. The chances of going blank in the hall is eliminated or reduced to the barest minimum. Let us try a little analysis of how the memory works and how you can improve your memory.

- The first thing is that the Sensory Register catches information for you to judge if you should attend to it further. If so, this is moved to the
- Short-Term Memory (STM), i.e., a working memory that holds information for only twenty seconds or so and then transfers to the
- Long-Term Memory (LTM) that may permanently store everything you have ever learned.

Studying can serve to hold information in the STM for immediate use or can help to move information to long-term memory. Well-organized material and information that is meaningful, which 'connects' with prior learning, will be learned more quickly, encoded in LTM, and retained for future retrieval. Repetition and practice are essential for encoding material into short-term and long-term memory. Try to form a mental image of what you are trying to learn; see it, hear it in your mind in addition to saying it out loud. Verbal encoding procedures such as category clustering and concept mapping may be helpful when trying to learn lots of formulas, facts, or other such information. Keyword method involves recoding, relating, and retrieving. Your note-taking style and methods should be related to your memory capabilities. They should complement each other. Even if you have a good memory, you still need to take good notes because your memory can fade but written notes are permanent.

CHAPTER EIGHTEEN

Other Important Factors and Areas of Interest to Note

Success, real success in any endeavour (including academics) demands more from an individual than most people are willing to offer-not more than they are capable of offering.[136]

—James Roche, twentieth secretary of the Air Force

You Need To Be Enthusiastic

Enthusiasm is the propelling force necessary for climbing the ladder of success. The truth is that *you simply will not go far without enthusiasm; neither will you go far if that is all you have.* You need action-packed enthusiasm. Is that clear? You should also know that enthusiasm is contagious and so is the lack of it. There is a saying that enthusiasm can achieve in one day what it takes centuries to achieve by reason.

Look into your daily affair; you will observe that you rarely support the things you support with equal measure of the enthusiasm with which you oppose the things you oppose. True or false? Enthusiasm is a good engine, but it needs intelligence for a driver. You need to understand that years put wrinkles on the skin, but lack of enthusiasm wrinkles the soul.[137] You also need to appreciate that enthusiasm and persistence can make an average person appear superior while indifference and lethargy can make a superior person appear average. You must have enthusiasm for your study and life generally, or life is not going to have a lot of enthusiasm for you. The question now is since *both enthusiasm and pessimism are contagious, which one do you spread? It is important in the pursuit of excellence!* 'Today is life—the only life you are sure of. Make the most of today. Get interested in something. Shake yourself awake. Develop a hobby. Let the winds of enthusiasm sweep through you. Live today with gusto,'[138] so says Dale Carnegie.

Eliminate Inefficiencies

Eliminate any form of inefficiency and redundancy. Cut through the complexities of your schedule and keep it simple and relevant. Remember the KISS principle articulated by Kelly Johnson:[139] Keep It Simple, Stupid, meaning that most systems work best if they are kept simple rather than made complex, therefore simplicity should be a key goal in design and unnecessary complexity should be avoided.

Complexity is proven to be a great enemy of excellence. Experiences show that simple, focused plans are more achievable. For instance, making a reading schedule that you will read five subjects or courses a day will land you in achieving nothing at the end of the day. It is better for you to make a schedule for, say, two subjects or courses a day for maximum output. Leverage your vital few and minimize your trivial many. Its result is faster and more efficient. Life rewards those who seize their time and take action. Excellence belongs to those who act instead of giving excuses. Actions may sometimes get lost in intentions, but other people judge you by what you do, not what you meant to do. Act now!

Conquer

You also need to stand the test of time. You might get discouraging attitudes and remarks from people at different points in the course of pursuing your goal. Some will even criticize your good academic performance, but do not be surprised. It can happen, but that should tell you that you are ahead of them so you should keep moving forward. Your attitude to such dispositions can make or mar you. No matter what, you should never allow people's irrelevant attitudes and remarks to weigh you down. It should not deter you at all. It should rather boost your motivation. It should make you perform better, and even perform better than you are already doing. This attitude will make you happier and more resilient. Adversity should be used as a time to identify opportunities to improve, learn, and grow. With the right attitude, roadblocks can be turned into stepping-stones. Know the things that are non-negotiable to you. These are the things that you should never compromise (your goal which is academic excellence). Excellent performers do not settle for what conditions force upon them. Achievers are known to be bold and faithful to their goals. Rise courageously above the crowd and then create new conditions for success by blazing new trails.

Delight in the Discomfort of Pursuing Your Goal

Studying can be seen as discomfort because it takes a lot from you, it demands that you sacrifice some of those things you enjoy doing, but it is better to keep your momentum even amidst the discomfort, and even delight in it! Discomfort allows you to keep your momentum and gives you a healthy alertness. Taking delight in your study despite the discomfort makes you more relaxed and somehow you get used to it. It helps you stay on track and thrive, rather than remaining defensive and merely passing. When you feel you are cruising to victory, take a look around—not only at yourself, but also your classmates. Observing the attitude of high flyers and achievers, even in other departments, will keep you humble and focused on improving yourself. High achievers are never satisfied and never complacent. Live beyond the status quo; always focus on the next level. Your goals should force changes, require tough actions, and inspire bold actions. Those that are easy to achieve are not big enough and will not allow you to get to the next level. Imagine scoring straight As in a term or semester. Do you think it is impossible? Wake up! Your classmates target it and some achieve it. I had once targeted that and succeeded in scoring As and just one B. You also can do the same. You even stand a better chance with this guide. I did not have an opportunity of reading this guide when I was in school.

Have Positive Attitude and Positive Influences

Use and believe in strong work ethics. Believe that effort, study time, and self-discipline will help propel you to the top of the ladder of academic excellence. Your decision to study any course will make you put in the required effort and you will excel. Make a decision that you are going to get the maximum benefit for your time in school. If you commence a subject or course with the mind-set that you will fail it, you probably will hate it and perform poorly. Positive attitude comes with positive influence. You have to be in love and at peace with your subjects or courses. Always think positively and work hard towards achieving those positive thoughts.

Declare Your Greatness

Your mouth has the power to create, so establish positive confessions and declare them out loud daily. Since our words frame how we think and feel, verbalize only the best. It amounts to suicide if you keep speaking negatively, having negative thoughts, and having negative feelings. You will sooner than later start believing it. Talk your way into achieving your goals.

The G-Factor

God, in his wisdom, has so much empowered man to rule the world around him and beyond, but it is the responsibility of man, not God, to utilize or explore that potential. Your greatest opportunity in life to develop capacity to explore these huge potentials is when you are in school and that is the best way to appreciate and thank God for such endowment in you. Without God, you will not be alive to read this. Always acknowledge his blessings in your affairs.

SECTION FIVE

Achievement

CHAPTER NINETEEN
Achieving Academic Excellence

The will to win, the desire to succeed, the urge to reach your full potential . . . these are the keys that will unlock the door to personal excellence.[140]

—Eddie Robinson (1919-2007), American football coach

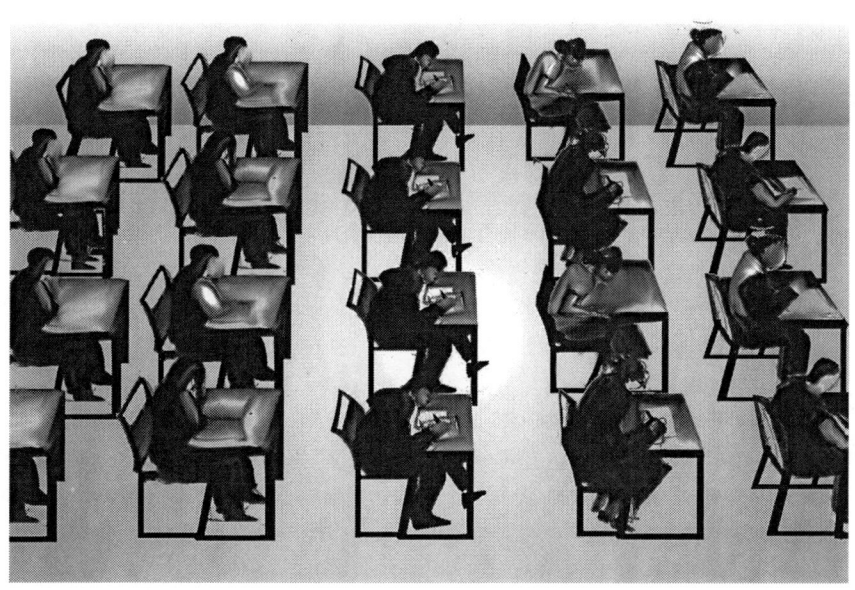

'*Destiny is a not a matter of chance. It is a matter of choice. It is not something to be waited for, but rather something to be achieved,*'[141] remarked William Jennings Bryan. Fight the examination battle with confidence, then you discover that winning is just easy. This confidence is built with the five Ps of success: Proper Preparation Prevents Poor Performance. It is important to note that *battles are really won or lost at the stage of preparation*. Brian Tracy said, '*All successful people, men and women, are big dreamers. They imagine*

what their future could be, ideal in every respect, and then they work every day toward their distant vision, that goal or purpose.'[142] Examination time is really the time for you to display what you have learnt without consulting any text or note. You can only make reference to your brain. Before the examination, I assume you have read all the necessary materials you need to. So this is the time to 'harvest your fruit'. Some students do not do well in examinations, not really because they did not read, but because they enter the hall *unorganized!* They have disjointed and unorganized ideas and information in their brains. This usually emanates from tension. They get tensed up in the examination hall and this may result in memory failure or uncoordinated approach to answering questions. This earns them *unexpected bad grades*. I refer to this failure as unexpected because the person feels he knows the answer to the questions, but the truth remains that the teacher will not go into your head to reveal what you know. He can only grade you based on what you wrote.

Examinations and tests are like battles, and how you prepare for them will determine not only your success or failure but the extent. So it is not only good to read, but also important

- **To view a test or examination as a challenge or opportunity to perform, not as a punishment.** Review extensively before you go to the examination hall.
- **That you learn to anticipate the trajectory of the questions that will appear in the examination.** Imagine possible examination questions and proffer answers to them. You can try my method. I imagine and set possible examination questions for myself in every course, both theory and subjective. And believe me, most of those questions do appear in the examinations, maybe in some rephrased form but having the same import. In this case you can say I have an edge. So try it, it will really help you a lot.
- **That you summarize your work.** You need to do a summary of each chapter. When a course is concluded, you should also do an overall summary. Generally, your summary should include the major topics covered such as major theorems, problems solved, major methods employed, techniques used in developing the theories and solving problems, typical examples considered, important assignments, quiz problems. Those problems have a high probability of appearing in the examination. At the end of each topic, think

of the meaning, the interconnections, significance, and possible variations. You can use a diagram to represent complex relationships. You can also use acronyms, whichever that works better for you. You also gain mastery of the topic by practicing problems until you are confident that you understand how the formula or principle works in all possible cases.

- **That you get to the examination hall early enough to get seated, settled, and relaxed.**
- **That you take 30-60 seconds out, sit back, and relax.** Try some relaxation techniques such as tense-relax your biceps and breathe deeply.
- **That you review all the questions before attempting any question. Read all the instructions and allocate your time properly.** Read the questions carefully. Highlight the buzzwords or phrases.
- **That you answer the easier questions first.**
- **That you manage your anxiety as that can render your efforts futile**. Avoid negative thoughts since such will increase your anxiety. Try not to exaggerate the importance or significance of the examination. See it as normal routine test of knowledge. Weeks before your examination, you must go over your texts, try to summarize the material into one or a few pages. Study your summary until you become very familiar with it, especially the highlighted points, your notes, assignments, and the like. Also ensure that you understand and remember every part. Do not be guessing while you are about to enter the hall. Confirm whatever it is because that might be the first question to confront you and could be a compulsory question too.
- **That you be conscious of time in the examination hall.** Sometimes you might know what to write but seem to have limited time to write them. This means that you did not manage your time well. Maybe you were so relaxed thinking out things to write, but that might result in your not attempting all the questions. So my advice to you from my personal experience here is this: attempt the easier questions first, do not waste all the time trying to think out what to write. Write those ideas that are flowing without much thought. Leave enough space depending on the magnitude of what you think that you still need to add. You can leave up to a page or more so you could come back to it after attempting the

other questions, but do not forget. This way, you will attempt all questions, write all you intend to and also beat the time. It is my style and it is very effective!

- **That you learn how to organize and present your answers logically and convincingly in examinations and tests.** So what you have learned needs to be digested, organized, and memorized for future use, which includes examinations.
- **That you write to convince.** Most time you hear students complain that they got an unsatisfactory grade after writing an assumed 'simple examination'. But the problem with such students is that, yes, they had an idea or sketchy hint about that topic. What they think they knew was too shallow to fetch them the mark they expected. I used to experience this with some courses I expected to make As but ended up scoring 68, that is, 2 points off my target. I did feel bad a lot of times. I got such results seven times. I then asked myself what the problem was. Because those examinations I considered easy. I told myself that maybe I was not writing all that was required of me. Since then, I have developed a habit of answering questions without reservation. Cite examples from text, from the lecture notes, teacher's example while teaching, make illustrations, and leave some space after answering each question so that I could include any additional idea I remember. What I am saying here is that it is better to exhaustively answer a question than doing otherwise. But you need to be very fast as well since you do not have all the time in the world.
- **That you try and review your answers before submission.** Normally you will be able to correct one or two mistakes. This will make your score much better. Remember it is the score that matters, not how early you turn in your script. *'The minute you settle for less than you deserve, you get even less than you settled for,'*[143] according to Maureen Dowd. And Terry Josephson assures you that *'the more you prepare, the luckier you appear'*.[144]
- **That you always monitor your health status.** You should always check your health status to ensure that you do not develop any problems during or around the examination period.

CHAPTER TWENTY

Take That Decision; You Can Do It

Somehow I cannot believe that there are any heights that cannot be scaled by a man who knows the secrets of making dreams come true. This special secret, it seems to me, can be summarized in four Cs. They are curiosity, confidence, courage, and constancy, and the greatest of all is confidence. When you believe in a thing, believe in it all the way, implicitly and unquestionably.[145]

—Walt Disney

Yes. A lot has been said in this book. The guide has been outlined, but I need sincere answers from you here:

- Is climbing the ladder to academic excellence really too difficult for you to try?
- Are the things required to get there really outrageous?
- Are you incapable of achieving it?
- Are you too dull to do it?

Of course not! The 1776 American Declaration of Independence states, '... *We hold these truths to be self evident that all men are created equal* . . .'[146] This simply implies that if anyone has done it, then you can do it. If anyone should do it, it is you! You see that these things are not really such a big deal. So I need you to convince yourself that *you* can make the *difference*. Dorthea Brand (1893-1948), who was a well-respected writer and editor in New York, stated, '*All that is necessary to break the spell of inertia and frustration is this; act as if it were impossible to fail.*'[147] Inability to make a decision makes one miserable. Being decisive is an absolute key to a successful life. Every accomplishment, great or small, starts with a decision. Decide to make it happen! Nothing great and outstanding was ever done without a decision.

James Hightower said that *'there is nothing in the middle of the road but yellow stripes and dead armadillos'*.[148] It is most dangerous to be in the middle of the road where you say 'I know I will pass, I will not just fail'. This is simply not good enough. You need to have a definite grade in mind. Passing can fetch you grades between E and A. It depends on the one you really decide to achieve. When you are decisive about your grade, you accept no excuses, only results. Indecisiveness has caused more failures than lack of intelligence or ability. You know why it seems that you do not know what to do? It is because you have not made some real decisions. Remain indecisive and you will never grow or get to the top of the ladder of excellence. Joseph Newton said, *'Not what we have but what we use, not what we see, but what we choose—these things that mar or bless human happiness.'*[149] Herbert Prochnow said, *'There is a time when we must firmly choose the course which we will follow, or the relentless drift of events will make the decision for us.'*[150] Indecision affects every facet of our lives. The book of James in the Holy Bible says, 'A double-minded man is unstable in all his ways.' Too many people go through life without knowing what they want, but feeling sure they do not have it.

Do not be a wheelbarrow, trailer, or canoe that needs to be pushed, pulled, or paddled to move. Edgar Roberts said, *'Every human mind is a great slumbering power until awakened by a keen desire and a definite resolution to do.'*[151] Decide to do something now to make your academic life better. The choice is yours.

David Ambrose said, *'If you have the will to win, you have achieved half your success; if you do not; you have achieved half your failure.'*[152] You cannot get your head above water if you never stick your neck out. It is better to be a lion for a day than a sheep all your life. Being destined for greatness requires you to take risks and confront great hazards. It is an irrefutable fact that you will always miss 100% of the shot that you do not take. No one reaches the top without daring.

Success favours the gallant. David Magoney advised that *'you should refuse to join the cautious crowd that plays not to lose. Play to win'*. Ronald Reagan, the 40th president of USA and 33rd Governor of California said *'The future doesn't belong to the fainthearted; it belongs to the brave'*.[153]

As stated above, you now know that to move from where you are, you must decide where you would rather be. Bertrand Russell said, *'Nothing is so exhausting as indecision and nothing is so futile.*'[154] Maurice Witzer also asserts that '*you seldom get what you go after unless you know in advance what you want*'.[155] Do you know that a single act creates a ripple effect that can be felt many miles and people away? *All changes start with one person, one thought, one word, one action.* Change your world starting with your academics with just one small act of *reading*. Your goal is not to change the world, but to change your life and the lives of those whose paths you cross. That way, the society will be changed and so also the world at large. *The same amount of time is required for a positive act and a negative one.* Make a positive change every day in your academic life. As an achiever, you must be the difference maker. Making positive changes reinforces this. You should always pursue excellence for you and the people around you. Your attitude to life and your academic work is what will come back to you. The ability to choose your attitude is a gift and a huge responsibility. You should always *think excellence*! I want you to know that you are the conductor of your own thoughts. No one else can control them for you. Your mind is a magnet. Only you can create your own positive attitude and, by so doing, attract things of a similar disposition. All you need to do now is to mentally reframe those challenges to enable you view them more as opportunities to make a change. True commitment never rests; keep pushing. Your responsibility as a student includes always pushing to achieve your set goal. An achiever never stops treading the path to success until he gets to the top of the ladder.

Your focus is a magnet for your life. Look for excellence in all you do and excellence will find you. The things we focus on create a magnet for our lives by attracting similar things. A person who focuses on excellence will thus be very likely to find it. Focusing on positive aspects of life attracts 'luck'. Their focus and preparation will put them in the right place at the right time. Hard work is the best predictor of luck . . . and excellence. A positive focus should be combined with hard work to achieve excellence. Hard work can yield defining moments for you, and also defining excellence! So what do you do now? Think excellence, and work excellence!

CHAPTER TWENTY-ONE

Success and Smiles at Last

Nobody who ever gave his best regretted it.[156]

—George Halas (1895-1983), coach, owner, and pioneer in professional American football

Anthony Robbins said, '*I've continued to recognize the power individuals have to change virtually anything and everything in their lives in an instant. I've learned that the resources we need to turn our dreams into reality are within us, merely waiting for the day when we decide to wake up and claim our birthright.*'[157]

Any time you sincerely want to make a change, the first thing you must do is to raise your standards. This really works! I am a witness and I also personally experienced it. When I scored As and a B grade in a semester, it was because I raised my standard. I changed what I demanded of myself. In the previous semesters, when my target was 4.7 or 4.8 cumulative grade point (GP) per semester, I scored 4.29, 4.5, and the like. However, when I targeted 5, I made 4.89 and 4.72. You see how it works? The more you demand of yourself, the more you work to achieve your dream so that even if you do not exactly attain your goal, it will not be too far. Since my second year in the university, I had a diary where I wrote down all my courses, created a column for anticipated grades and another column for actual grades. It happened that I got most of the grades I had anticipated. Commit yourself to excellence from the start. No legacy is as rich as excellence. The quality of your life and academic achievements will be a direct proportion to your commitment to excellence.

In summary, failure in academic activities can be prevented if the following are considered:

- Set goals on what you desire to achieve and map out appropriate strategies.
- Read textbooks, journals, and other educative materials.
- Visit the library to supplement your personal textbooks.
- Do not depend on your notes alone; read other relevant texts.
- Read other books outside your field to achieve versatility.
- Create time to study outside the classroom.
- Learn to communicate effectively in written and spoken English.
- Attend classes regularly.
- Ask questions during lectures/classes.
- Establish a cordial relationship with your lecturers/teachers.
- Be optimistic.
- Be determined.
- Do not waste all your time watching television, movies, and attending disco parties, pinging, and other distracting activities.
- Do not be too playful.
- Avoid bad group.

Hard Work Pays in Everything; Academics Not an Exception

The theme of this write-up, as you can see, is that *'hard work is the ultimate in getting to the top of the ladder of academic excellence'*. According to Steve Pavlina, *'When you live for a strong purpose, then hard work is not an option. It is a necessity.'*[158] For Thomas Alva Edison, the American inventor and businessman who developed many devices that greatly influenced life around

SUCCESS AND SMILES AT LAST

the world, including the phonograph, the motion picture camera, and a long-lasting, practical electric light bulb, *'There is no substitute for hard work.'* [159] Lakshmi Mittal, CEO of ArcelorMittal, the world's largest steelmaker, India's richest man with net worth of $16 billion, believes, *'Hard work certainly goes a long way. These days a lot of people work hard, so you have to make sure you work even harder and really dedicate yourself to what you are doing and setting out to achieve.'* [160] Thomas Jefferson, an American Founding Father, the principal author of the Declaration of Independence (1776), and the third president of the United States (1801-1809), declared, *'I'm a great believer in luck and I find the harder I work, the more I have of it.'* [161]

- Tell yourself today that you will no more accept just any grade
- That you are better than some very poor grades
- That you can have the best result
- That your score can be among the highest in each course
- You cannot forever be average.
- The God that created you did not create you to be just average
- He made you whole so why are you limiting yourself?
- Say I can no longer accept just let my people go grade (E).
- Say I have outgrown poor grades!

All these top achievers owe their successes to hard work.

If you make up your mind about the things you would no longer entertain in your academic life, all the things you would no longer tolerate, and back it up with the necessary action, I assure you that you will have great testimonies to make. This includes overcoming the obstacles on your way going up the ladder and all the things that you aspire to achieve and become. It takes less time to do something right than it does to explain why you got it wrong in the first place. You will forever have to keep explaining the reason for your poor performance to your parents, guardian, siblings, friends, employer, and children. So keep looking up towards attaining your goals. Work towards it by putting in all the necessary efforts. This will make you achieve your aim and then you will be happy you did. Excellence is sweet! You will get to the top of the ladder of academic excellence with your teeth shining out as you beam with *smiles* due to your outstanding *success*!

CHAPTER TWENTY-TWO

Keep the Flag Flying High: Personal Development

Personal development is your springboard to personal excellence. Ongoing, continuous, non-stop personal development literally assures you that there is no limit to what you can accomplish.[162]

—Brian Tracy

While pursuing your academic success, it is also very important that you keep developing yourself for life after school, in the workplace, family, as a leader, an entrepreneur, and the like. Personal development does not necessarily occur simply because you passed through a higher institution of learning. It comprises the sum total of your personality, attitudes and disposition, general outlook, carriage, decorum, and all those attributes that prepare you for a life of success and leadership wherever you find yourself. Such 'packaging', intended to promote and present you to others in a way intended to ensure appeal and acceptance, matters a lot and that is why personal development is paramount. A wonderful product that is badly packaged will have the same effect as a bad product in the marketplace. The packaging of a product is what attracts people first before reading or testing the content.

So in as much as you strive to be academically sound, it is also necessary that you look beyond mere paper achievement for avenues for personal development that encompasses good character formation, skill acquisition, and the like. You can start developing yourself now by reading development books, leadership books, attending seminars, reading autobiographies or biographies of world icons, listening to world leaders in different fields, and learning from their wealth of experiences. This is why I stated above that you need to read other books for versatility.

You must not have personal experience of every situation on earth before you learn. You must not make every mistake so as to learn from them. You need to learn from other people's mistakes and successes. For general life success, you should set your goals, which may be short—or long-term; set priorities and achieve total success. I am sure you have learnt that knowing clearly what you want will set you on the right path from the very beginning of your journey to success. What are the important goals in your career and your life? How can you set priorities, keep a balance, and achieve your total success? You might wonder what total success actually is.

I choose to agree with Lee J. Colan:

> Total Success = Good health, physical well-being
> PLUS Positive attitude in mind, emotions, and personality
> PLUS Good academic performance
> PLUS Active social activities, personal skills, leadership
> PLUS Sufficient financial, business, and other real-life skills

A four-year or more university program should train you to be a professional, mature, and well-developed individual, but to achieve total success, other parts of life such as health, social life, and friendships need not be totally ignored. The emphasis is that while in school, your studies should take a front seat. Integrating all the parts together is the right way to a successful, happy, and meaningful life and future.

It was Woodrow Wilson (1856-1924), the twentieth president of the United States, who posited, *'You are not here merely to make a living. You are here in order to enable the world to live more amply, with greater vision, with a finer spirit of hope and achievement. You are here to enrich the world, and you impoverish yourself if you forget the errand.'* [163]

Becoming a graduate is not all that matters in the higher institution. Yes! It is pertinent to work hard to obtain a very good certificate that will make you competitive in the global labour market; acquire a wide scope of knowledge and skills necessary for effective living and attain physical, academic, and moral developments. However, apart from a good certificate, there are other crucial things you need to do to get the total packaging of a graduate right.

Nowadays, many graduates cannot be distinguished from non-graduates in the society. In the golden days of yore, graduates were treated with so much respect because they were believed to be very knowledgeable and prospective leaders. Acquire the habits that are conducive to continuous self-development, not only in your discipline, but in the liberal arts, sciences, music, and other fields of endeavour. You do not need to be an expert in all fields, but a little knowledge of all will distinguish you from the pack. That is why higher institutions offer courses outside your immediate discipline. In Igbo language, a graduate is referred to as *mahadum*, meaning 'him that knows it all'. Graduates were not seen just as people who attended higher institutions, but also people who knew a lot more than their counterparts who had no such opportunity.

Sadly, it will be difficult to make such salubrious references to graduate from many institutions of higher learning at this time. Therefore, the only thing that actually distinguishes you from the pack is the quality of your education—what you have to offer your nation and the world at large. In order to rightly 'package' yourself as a graduate, you need to check yourself for the following distinguishing characteristics of a sound graduate:

(a) Ability to defend your certificate.

> In present-day Nigeria, for instance, a lot of people graduate with results they often cannot defend. This way, they end up messing the reputation of their alma mater. Actually, the possessor of this type of result might have actually earned it but had forgotten everything simply because he or she crammed just to pass the examinations. Such study style fetch you a pass but cause you serious embarrassment when you are called upon to defend your degree in the future. If you are in the league of those that hire people to impersonate in their examinations or those that buy examination results, you are not likely to be able to defend that result anywhere tomorrow.
>
> What I am saying here in essence is, first, it is very good to make a wonderful result. That is what will recommend you to be tested to confirm your abilities. Second, you should adopt a reading style that will

engender retention. I feel challenged when I hear older persons refer to what they learnt in school. How much of your previous classwork can you recollect now without consulting textbooks? If you were suddenly asked to repeat the examination you wrote last semester and scored an A, can you in all honesty write it now and still score the same grade without any reference? At least you should not forget everything. Find a reading method that will help you retain most of the things you learnt. Employ the gradual method that enables storage of information in your long-term memory. That way you will be able and capable of defending your good certificate anywhere.

(b) Good dress sense.

Another wonderful thing a graduate should be conscious of is his physical appearance. *'What we (you) put on our (your) body is very important in getting along with people. Poor dressing can damage your relationship with others. People can belittle you due to your appearance in a given gathering. One can be ashamed of introducing you as a friend, husband, or wife due to your appearance . . . once the appearance is shabby or tattered, most people do not bother to be more intimate with that person even if he/she has finer qualities,'*[164] says David Iluebe. *'Dress for success, image is very important. People judge you by the way you look on the outside,'*[165] says Brian Tracy.

You should dress as a product of a higher institution who is worthy in character and learning. Your dressing is meant to be admired. I am not talking about buying new or expensive clothes, but a correct and neat combination of what you have. You should always look smart and clean. A graduate is not supposed to wear a dress twice without washing and ironing it. It makes you look shabby and spread an awful odour. For men, you should always shave clean and also mind your stockings. For women, you need to take care of your hair as that has a lot to do with your look and people's impression of you. Your hair can make you look younger or older, smart or dull, responsible or irresponsible.

Also note that there is a dress code for different kind of events and places. It is wrong to mix up any of them as that will make you odd. Try dressing like a mad person and compare it with dressing in a smart corporate outfit. Incorporated here also is how you walk, especially for ladies. Do not just lift your leg and place it in front but make an organized movement. Walk in a way that people will turn to admire. Exude confidence in your step! It is another distinguishing attribute. If you want to confirm how important good dress sense is, look up corporate events, national and international conferences, check out the national assembly sessions. Dressing well is a good business. The advice here is dress right, clean, and smart!

(c) Table manners.

Table manners could distinguish you from the pack. It is very important, but people usually ignore it all in the name of trying not to behave like the Americans or Europeans. It is silly! You can eat in your house anyhow you like, but at world-class events, you should be able to use your cutleries properly. Look, there is no pretentiousness in having good table manners. It is something every graduate ought to know. In the 1960s and 1970s when students were eating at the school refectory, they were trained on table manners. You do not eat with your hands for instance. You are meant to use the cutleries correctly. This is important to avoid embarrassing not only yourself but your friends and colleagues at corporate lunch and dinner sessions. My Uncle recently told me about a lady at a lunch session they had in Lagos with foreign partners who held her fork on the right hand and poised as if set for a fight to nab a rattle snake. It was obvious she didn't know the table etiquettes. The point I am trying to communicate here is this: as a graduate, you should know how to use your cutleries and eat comfortably with them. If you do not know how, start learning it now or you will be terribly embarrassed. Planning for a great future entails preparing yourself like a great man. We have our African culture of eating things with hands, but I am sure that you now eat with spoons. Just like we acquire Western education and aspire for white collar jobs, we need to learn their accompaniments like having good table manners especially for corporate events. If you want to attend those big conferences, nationally and internationally, learn the etiquette now!

(d) How to talk.

A graduate is always expected to talk with some culture and sophistication. It is necessary that a graduate differentiates himself by talking like one who acquired some education. English language is not our mother tongue, but whenever you need to use it, try and produce organized sounds, speak with some magnificence. Do not just open your mouth and talk. I am not saying that you should twist your mouth because you want to talk. Talk sensibly and not shout like an angry tout. Ensure that you use correct grammar and tenses.

(e) Be versatile.

As a graduate, it will be good you have some knowledge of most things. Use the internet, read newspapers, listen to news. Be abreast with global trends, fads, buzzwords, and information on a wide range of issues. Read to enhance your knowledge and exploit new opportunities. Versatility is encouraged even in the universities. That is why in some institutions, if you score straight As but fail a course, your cumulative might be 4.8, but they would not give you a first class. The belief is that a first-class student should know a little of everything, even outside your field.

Having said all these, pay attention to the following extract from President Obama's speech at a back-to-school event at Wakefield High School in Arlington, Virginia, USA, on 8 September 2009.

> *Now, I've given a lot of speeches about education, and I've talked about responsibility a lot. I've talked about teachers' responsibility for inspiring students and pushing you to learn. I've talked about your parents' responsibility for making sure you stay on track, and you get your homework done, and do not spend every waking hour in front of the TV or with the Xbox. I've talked a lot about your government's responsibility for setting high standards, and supporting teachers and principals, and turning around schools that are not working where students are not getting the opportunities that they deserve.* ***But at the end of the day, we can have the most dedicated teachers, the most supportive parents, the best schools in the world, and none of it will make a difference—none of it will matter—unless all of you fulfil your responsibilities: unless you show up to those schools, unless you pay attention to those teachers, unless you listen to your parents and grandparents and other adults and put in the hard work it takes to succeed. And that's what I want***

to focus on today: the responsibility each of you has for your education. *I want to start with the responsibility you have to yourself.*

Every single one of you has something that you are good at. Every single one of you has something to offer. And you have a responsibility to yourself to discover what that is. That's the opportunity an education can provide. Maybe you could be a great writer; maybe even good enough to write a book or articles in the newspaper. But you might not know it until you write that English paper—that English class that is assigned to you. Maybe you could be an innovator or an inventor; maybe even good enough to come up with the next iPhone or the new medicine or vaccine. But you might not know it until you do your project for your science class. Maybe you could be a mayor or a senator or a Supreme Court justice. But you might not know that until you join student government or the debate team. ***And no matter what you want to do with your life, I guarantee that you'll need an education to do it.*** *You want to be a doctor or a teacher or a police officer, you want to be a nurse or an architect, a lawyer or a member of our military, you are going to need a good education for every single one of those careers.* ***You cannot drop out of school and just drop into a good job.***

You've got to train for it and work for it and learn for it. *And this is not just important for your own life and your own future. What you make of your education will decide nothing less than the future of this country. The future of America depends on you. What you're learning in school today will determine whether we as a nation can meet our greatest challenges in the future. You will need the knowledge and problem-solving skills you learn in science and math to cure diseases like cancer and AIDS, and to develop new energy technologies and protect our environment. You will need the insights and critical thinking skills you gain in history and social studies to fight poverty and homelessness, crime and discrimination, and make our nation more fair and more free. You will need the creativity and ingenuity you develop in all your classes to build new companies that will create new jobs and boost our economy. We need every single one of you to develop your talents and your skills and your intellect so you can help us old folks solve our most difficult problems. If you do that, if you quit on school, you are not just quitting on yourself, you're quitting* *on your country. Now, I know it's not always easy to do well in school. I know a lot of you have challenges in your lives right now that can make it hard to focus on your schoolwork. I get it. I know what it is like. My father left my family when I was 2 years old, and I was raised by a single mom who had to work and had struggled at times to pay the bills and was not always able to give us the things that other kids had. There were times when I missed having a father in my life. There were times when I was lonely and I felt like I did not fit in.*

So I was not always as focused as I should have been on school. But I was—I was fortunate. I got a lot of second chances and I had the opportunity to go to college and law school and follow my dreams. My wife, our first lady, Michelle Obama, she has a similar story. Neither of her parents had gone to college, and they did not have a lot of money. But they worked hard, and she worked hard, so that she could go to the best schools in this country.

But some of you might not have those advantages. Maybe you do not have adults in your life who give you the support that you need. Maybe someone in your family has lost their job, and there's not enough money to go around. Maybe you live in a neighborhood where you do not feel safe, or have friends who are pressuring you to do things you know are not right. **But at the end of the day, the circumstances of your life—what you look like, where you come from, how much money you have, what you've got going on at home—none of that is an excuse for neglecting your homework or having a bad attitude in school. That is no excuse for talking back to your teacher or cutting class or dropping out of school. There is no excuse for not trying.**

Where you are right now does not have to determine where you will end up. No one's written your destiny for you. Because here in America you write your own destiny, you make your own future . . . That is why today I am calling on each of you to set your own goals for your education and do everything you can to meet them.

Your goal can be something as simple as doing all your homework, paying attention in class, or spending some time each day reading a book. *Maybe you will decide to get involved in an extracurricular activity or volunteer in your community . . . . Maybe you will decide to take better care of yourself so you can be more ready to learn. But whatever you resolve to do, I want you to commit to it. I want you to really work at it.*

I know that sometimes you get that sense from TV that you can be rich and successful without any hard work; that your ticket to success is through rapping or basketball or being a reality TV star. Chances are, you are not going to be any of those things.

The truth is, being successful is hard. You will not love every subject that you study. You will not click with every teacher that you have. Not every homework assignment will seem completely relevant to your life right at this minute. And you will not necessarily succeed at everything the first time you try.

That is OK. Some of the most successful people in the world are the ones who have had the most failures . . . These people succeeded because they understood that you cannot let your failures define you; you have to let your failures teach you; you have to let them show you what to do differently the next time . . . If you **get a bad grade, that does not mean you are stupid. It just means you need to spend more time studying.**

No one's born being good at all things. You become good at things through hard work. *You are not a varsity athlete the first time you play a new sport. You do not hit every note the first time you sing a song. You've got to practice. The same principle applies to your schoolwork. You might have to do a math problem a few times before you get it right. You might have to read something a few times before you understand it. You definitely have to do a few drafts of a paper before it is good enough to hand in. Do not be afraid to ask questions. Do not be afraid to ask for help when you need it. I do that every day. Asking for help isn't a sign of weakness, it is a sign of strength, because it shows you have the courage to admit when you do not know something and that, then, allows you to learn something new. So find an adult that you trust—a parent, a grandparent, or* *a teacher, a coach or a counselor—and ask them to help you stay on track to meet your goals.*

And even when you are struggling, even when you're discouraged, and you feel like other people have given up on you, do not ever give up on yourself. Because when you give up on yourself, you give up on your country. *The story of America isn't about people who quit when things got tough. It is about people who kept going, who tried harder, who loved their country too much to do anything less than their best.*

It's the story of students who sat where you sit 250 years ago and went on to wage a revolution and they founded this nation—young people; students who sat where you sit 75 years ago who overcame a depression and won a world war; who fought for civil rights and put a man on the moon; students who sat where you sit 20 years ago who founded Google, Twitter, and Facebook and changed the way we communicate with each other.

So today I want to ask all of you, what's your contribution going to be? What problems are you going to solve? What discoveries will you make? What will a president who comes here in 20 or 50 or 100 years say about what all of you did for this country?

But you've got to do your part too. So I expect all of you to get serious this year. I expect you to put your best effort into everything you do. I expect great things from each of you. So do not let us down. Do not let your family down or your country down. Most of all, do not let yourself down. Make us all proud.[166]

Whoa! That was a great speech. Such a fully packaged speech from a world-class icon and brand—the first African American president of the United States of America—should tell you that achieving academic excellence is a beautiful experience you live with all your life. It is not what you can just attain without working for it.

CHAPTER TWENTY-THREE

Conclusion

This book set out to offer practical and hands-on solutions to students in their desire to excel within the constraints imposed by the Nigerian deteriorating academic environment. It proffers remedial measures to address those actions and inactions attributable to the students that conduce to the declining education standard in Nigeria as these are within the students' own control. These include focus, vision, planning, hard work, supported by the right attitude, motivation, and determination.

I started by stressing the need for the student to define his goal as this is the first step for every achiever. This helps to keep the student *focused* and avoid the numerous distractions that abound in school. Emphasis has been laid on the importance of precision in the articulation of academic goals by the student. The student needs to be forward looking to his goal, vision, and dreams. This goal could be defined better when the student is focused, appreciates how his or her academic journey started, believe that background and social status is not and can never be an obstacle to excellent academic achievement. As I explained in this book, one's background hardly determines one's future. You are the ultimate architect of your own fortune through God's help. No matter how bad your previous academic performance has been, you can start today. Make a change for a happy ending because you cannot buy back the past and no amount of reminiscing can change it. Just have a destination in mind. Like John Mason rightly remarked, 'The world makes room for a person of purpose, their words and actions demonstrates that they know where they are going.'

The falling standards of education in Nigeria were evidenced by the dismal performance of students at the ordinary level examinations namely WAEC and NECO over the past decade. While such exogenous factors as poor and inadequate infrastructure, uncompetitive, and poorly motivated teachers and

CONCLUSION

the like contribute in no small measure to the malaise, the fact remains that the student is his or her own greatest enemy or friend as the case may be. A lot of students engage in all sorts of distracting activities such as frequenting the nightclub, showing off, prostituting, belonging to criminal gangs, and the like while in school instead of focusing on their academic work. They engage in all manner of examination malpractice instead of reading their books. They deploy modern communication and computing technology to the detriment of their academic pursuits instead of knowledge enhancement. They prefer to spent their time watching movies and with the Xbox. They prefer to spend their time engaged in the social networking activities in platforms such as Facebook, Myspace, Twiter, Yahoo!, Google, 2go, Badoo, Twitter, WhatsApp, Instagram chats, and the like rather than deploying these tools for sourcing information to prepare better seminar papers, assignments, and projects. They choose to photocopy other student's assignments rather than painstakingly carrying out theirs. The cumulative effect of these is the production of ill-prepared and uncompetitive graduates, barely literate.

Also a lot of possible obstacles that could impede the student's attainment of his set academic objectives were discussed, with a view to identifying strategies that will assist the determined student break out from the low-achievement trap and actualize his goal. First, there is the 'transition shock' when a student transits from one academic level to another, with its many challenges, expectations, and realignment. The student is exposed to the possible challenges roommates, peers, and wannabes can pose against his academic goal. Practical solutions grounded in experience are offered to enable the student navigate these uncharted waters. I highlighted the need for a role model or mentor as that will go a long way in keeping the student on course I also brought to the fore the potential impediments to academic excellence likely to arise by perceptions, actions, and inactions. The grave danger of addictions to social networks, the destructive habit of procrastination, bad sleeping habits, bad eating habits, and other external factors that could stand between the student and his/her goal have been fully discussed and ways of addressing each of these proffered.

Without strong *determination, right attitudes, and positive motivation,* the attainment of a student's laudable goals will remain a pipe dream. The student needs to put in an effort beyond the usual to attain his or her goal of being a distinguished personality in Nigeria and the entire globe tomorrow. The end goal should always be the motivating factor. You as the student could become so important that the world would seek after you, and then you can become an idol or role model to so many, a source of inspiration to generations after you. The top of the ladder is inhabited by only great people. It is just like some class of people living in some prime real estates. It is not everybody that can afford to live there. It is for only those who can work hard and smart.

You would have discovered that there is a price to pay to be at the top. That price is determined by the height you want to attain. If you are primed for the top, then you have to pay a special price for that. That is to say that your *effort* is paramount if you must achieve your goal. Strive to overcome the obstacles on your way as you climb the academic ladder graciously and gloriously fly with great focus and precision. It has been clearly explained by John Mason that 'it is always bumpy, uphill road that leads to heights of greatness'. These efforts include eliminating your fear and limiting belief, forming good class attitudes such as going to class on time, paying attention when the class is in progress, taking good notes, asking reasonable questions, forming good study attitude that includes reviewing your notes before and after the class, managing your reading time well, forming good study group, getting help from teachers when you require any, optimizing your sweet spot, studying sufficiently to avoid rushing during examination, reading textbooks, and others that include exercising for at least fifteen minutes daily.

It is expected that with commensurate effort, you will be able to achieve your academic goal of getting to the top of the ladder to academic excellence. God will surely crown your efforts with a wonderful package of great accomplishments, peace, joy, and resounding success at the top of the ladder. You sure will be proud of your *achievements*.

At the top of the ladder of excellence, you cannot help but beam with *smiles*! Congratulations!

While you are smiling, remember the words of Marianne Williamson in her book *A Return to Love: Reflections on the Principles of a Course in Miracles*, 'Our deepest fear is not that we are inadequate. Our deepest fear is that we are powerful beyond measure. It is our light, not our darkness that most frightens us. We ask ourselves, who am I to be brilliant, gorgeous, talented, fabulous? Actually, who are you *not* to be? You are a child of God. Your playing small does not serve the world. There is nothing enlightened about

CONCLUSION

shrinking so that other people will not feel insecure around you. We are all meant to shine, as children do. We were born to make manifest the glory of God that is within us. It's not just in some of us; it's in everyone. And as we let our own light shine, we unconsciously give other people permission to do the same. As we are liberated from our own fear, our presence automatically liberates others.'[167]

References

1. National Bureau of Statistics, Federal Republic of Nigeria. Annual abstract of statistics (2007). Pg 67-92.
2. National Bureau of Statistics, Federal Republic of Nigeria. Annual abstract of statistics (2009), Pg 77-101.
3. B. L. Needham, R. Crosnoe, and C. Muller (2010). Academic Failure in Secondary School: The Inter-Related Role of Health Problems and Educational Context. Social Problem; 51(4): 569-586. Retrieved on 1/12/2010 from www.google.com/PMCID: PMC2846654 NIHMSID: NIHMS179490.
4. Burke T. (2010). 5 bad habits that affect academic performance. E-book.
5. Charles Nnamdi Anumudu (2010). Who will teach my child? Linco press, Nig.ltd.
6. Colan L. J. (2006). 7 Moments . . . That Define Excellent Leaders, Cornerstone Leadership Institute publishers.
7. Covey S R. (1990). The 7 habits of highly effective people, Powerful lessons in personal change, Simon & Schuster, New York.
8. Crosnoe Robert. High School Curriculum Track and Adolescent Association with Delinquent Friends. Journal of Adolescent Research. 2002b;17:144-168.
9. David Iluebe (2005). Immortal words of notable mortals. (Powerful quotations with biographical information). Ade-olu printers and publishers.
10. Educational Psychology, 71, 3-25. European Journal of Scientific Research.
11. Federal Ministry of Education: Ministerial platform on key achievements in commemoration of the first anniversary of president Goodluck Ebele Jonathan's administration, a paper presented by the Hon Minister of Education Prof. Ruqayyatu Ahmed Rufai'I.
12. Gardner J. N. and Jewler J. A. (1998). Your College Experience, Strategies for Success, Wadsworth Publishing Company.

13. Groccia J. E. (1992). The College Success Book, Glenbridge Publishing Ltd. in May/June 2003 ISSN 1450-216X Vol.52 No.3 (2011), pp. 406-412.
14. John Mason (2003). Know your limits, then ignore them. Bridge-Logos publishers Inc.
15. Laskey M. L. and Gibson P. W. (1997). College Study Strategies, Thinking and Learning, Allyn and Bacon, New York.
16. Le Foll, D. and Rascle, O. (2006). Failure: Influence of State-attributions and Attributional.
17. Meneghetti, C. and De Beni, R. (2010). Influence of motivational beliefs and strategies on recall task performance in elementary, middle and high school students. European Journal of Psychological Education 25:325-343. Retrieved on 1/12/2010 from *http://www.eurojournals.com/ ejsr.htmDOI 10.1007/s10212-010-0019-4*
18. Miller S. R. (1998). Shortcut: High School Grades as a Signal of Human Capital. Educational Evaluation and Policy Analysis. 20:299-311.
19. Miller S. R. (1998). Shortcut: High School Grades as a Signal of Human Capital. Educational Evaluation and Policy Analysis. 20:299-311.
20. Napoleon Hill (1960). Think and grow Rich, United States of America, combined Registry company.
21. Federal Ministry of Education Nigeria: Statistics of education in Nigeria (1999-2005). Statistics & NEMIS Branch. Pg 144-166.
22. Neff, K. D., Hsieh, Y. and Dejitterat, K. (2005). Self-compassion, Achievement Goals, and Coping with Academic Failure. Self and Identity, 4 263-287.
23. Nigeria: Digest of education statistics (2006-2010). Federal ministry of education, Nigeria.
24. Okpaluba C. (2009). Life after school. CEFARRD publishers.
25. Philosophy, Time Problem; 51(4): 569-586. Retrieved on 1/12/2010 from www.google.com/PMCID.
26. Richard J. Light (2001). Making the most of college, Harvard University Press, Third Printing.
27. Secondary School: The Inter-Related Role of Health Problems and Educational Context. Social Style. UFR APS Rennes, France N. C. Higgins.
28. W. Mitchell e-book: It is not what happens to you, it is what you do about it.
29. Weiner, B. (1979). A theory of motivation for some classroom experiences. Journal of Educational Psychology, 71, 3-25.

30. Weiner, B. (1985). An attributional theory of achievement motivation and emotion. Psychological Review, 92, 548-573.
31. Williamson M. *A Return to Love: Reflections on the Principles of A Course in Miracles*, Harper Collins, 1992. From Chapter 7, Section 3 (Pg. 190-191).

Endnotes

Introduction

1. *http://www.quoteworld.org/quotes/11283*
2. *http://www.quotes-clothing.com/opens-school-closes-prison-victor-hugo/*
3. *http://quotationsbook.com/quote/11841/*
4. *http://www.un.org/en/globalissues/briefingpapers/efa/quotes.shtml*
5. *http://www.whitehouse.gov/the_press_office/Fact-Sheet-Expanding-the-Promise-of-Education-in-America*
6. *http://www.whitehouse.gov/the-press-office/remarks-president-barack-obama-address-joint-session-congress*
7. *http://www.graduationwisdom.com/speeches/0067-schwarzenegger.htm*

Chapter One

8. *http://www.brainyquote.com/quotes/quotes/a/abrahamlin121354.html#F61tw8y3QerMDZhb.99*
9. Babalola, A. 2006. The Dwindling Standards of Education in Nigeria. First Distinguished Lecture Series of the Lead University, Ibadan.
10. Leadership and the Challenges of Higher Education in Nigeria—by Senator Babafemi Ojudu, October 31st, 2012 posted by NigerianMuse // Categories: Higher Education in Nigeria.
11. Times Higher Education World University Rankings 2012-2013.
12. http://www.4icu.org/topAfrica/
13. http://achievepace.com/best-nigerian-university-ranked-6340-in-the-world-2/
14. Leadership and the Challenges of Higher Education in Nigeria—by Senator Babafemi Ojudu, October 31st, 2012 posted by NigerianMuse // Categories: Higher Education in Nigeria.
15. Chinelo Ogoamaka Duze, 2011. Falling standard in Nigeria education: traceable to proper skills-acquisition in schools.
16. Anya OA (2003). Leadership, education, and the challenge of development in the 21st century. Vanguard, October 21: 26.
17. John U. Nwalor, 2012. Reviving Academic Standards in Nigerian Universities: Role of the Academia.

ENDNOTES

18. http://www.dailyschoolnews.com.ng/2012/05/20122013-jamb-official-cut-off-mark-for-nigeria-universities-polytechnics-and-college-of-education-20122013-latest-update.html
19. http://www.tribune.com.ng/news/top-stories/item/3545-jamb-releases-2014-utme-results-47-candidates-out-of-1-million-score-above-250/3545-jamb-releases-2014-utme-results-47-candidates-out-of-1-million-score-above-250
20. http://www.myunndreams.org/2013/05/jamb-releases-20132014-utme-results.html
21. Dr. J.U. Nwalor, 2010. "Reviving Academic Standards in Nigerian Universities: Role of the Academia". Education Workshop 2010.
22. John U. Nwalor, 2012. Reviving Academic Standards in Nigerian Universities: Role of the Academia.
23. http://ezinearticles.com/?Falling-Standard-Of-Education-In-Nigeria:-Who-Is-To-Be-Blame?&id=5230921

Chapter Two

24. *http://blog.gaiam.com/quotes/authors/lord-chesterfield-stanhope?page=2*
25. *http://ebookdirectory.com/dl/successbrand7.pdf*
26. *http://thinkexist.com/quotes/helen_keller/*
27. *http://www.worldofquotes.com/author/Fitzhugh+Dodson/1/index.html*
28. *http://www.famousquotes.com/show/1024594*
29. John M.(1999), Know your limits and then ignore them p. 51, insight publishing Group, Yale.
30. *http://blog.gaiam.com/quotes/topics/indecision*
31. *http://biblebrowser.com/philippians/3-14.htm*
32. *http://www.winwisdom.com/quotes/mark-victor-hansen/241219.aspx*
33. *http://www.frases-ingles.net/carl-sandburg/25149/there-are-people-who-want-to-be-everywhere-at-once/*
34. *http://www.dumb.com/quotes/goals-quotes/10/*
35. *http://ebookdirectory.com/dl/successbrand7.pdf*
36. *http://quotationsbook.com/quote/17155/*
37. *http://www.1-love-quotes.com/quote/18525*
38. *http://thinkexist.com/quotation/quality_questions_create_a_quality_life/7416.html*
39. *http://humanresources.about.com/od/workrelationships/a/quotes_goals.htm*
40. *http://blog.gaiam.com/quotes/authors/lord-chesterfield-stanhope?page=2*
41. *http://history1900s.about.com/od/ronaldreagan/a/Reagan-Quotes.htm*
42. *http://www.iwise.com/SeB92*

43. *http://thinkexist.com/quotation/be_like_a_postage_stamp-stick_to_one_thing_until/212120.html*
44. *http://lemmyc.hubpages.com/hub/How-to-harness-the-power-of-goal-setting*
45. *http://www.brainyquote.com/quotes/quotes/n/napoleonhi152853.html*
46. As quoted in *Diamond Power: Gems of Wisdom from America's Greatest Marketer* (2003) by Barry Farber, p. 53
47. *http://www.motivateus.com/rem-39.htm*

Chapter Three
48. *http://www.brainyquote.com/quotes/authors/a/alex_noble.html*
49. www.quotationspage.com/quote/24004.html
50. Malcolm Gladwell. Outliers. Learning 2009 Keynote - Outliers. November 9th, 2009.
51. *http://blog.gaiam.com/quotes/authors/rolf-jensen*
52. *http://www.brainyquote.com/quotes/quotes/m/margaretth114264.html*
53. *http://powertochange.com/life/quotesonsuccess/*
54. *http://www.goodreads.com/quotes/165556-the-past-does-not-equal-the-future*

Chapter Four
55. Willian S. the Twelfth Night (act ii, scene v) *http://www.william-shakespeare.info/quotes-quotations-play-twelfth-night.htm*
56. *http://www.briantracy.com/blog/business-success/planning-your-year-part-one/*
57. *http://www.idiomcenter.com/dictionary/as-you-make-your-bed-so-you-must-lie-in-it*
58. *http://meanttobehappy.com/you-have-to-do-your-own-growing-no-matter-how-tall-your-grandfather-was/*
59. Mohandas Karamchand Gandhi (2 October 1869-30 January *1948*),
60. *http://quotationsbook.com/quote/33654/*
61. *http://thinkexist.com/quotes/jim_rohn/*
62. *http://www.quotationspage.com/quote/31294.html*

Chapter Five
63. *http://www.thequotefactory.com/quote-by/ralph-waldo-emerson/the-world-makes-way-for-the-man/84403*
64. *http://www.brainyquote.com/quotes/quotes/z/zigziglar381977.html#0E9U12pkJ2tJ4ctL.99*

Chapter Six
65. *http://lesbrown.org/lesbrown.com/english/meet_lesbrown.html*

ENDNOTES

Chapter Seven
66. *http://quotationsbook.com/quote/20165/*
67. BETTY J. CAPPELLA, MARION WAGNER, and JULIA A. KUSMIERZ (1982), RELATION OF STUDY HABITS AND ATTITUDES TO ACADEMIC PERFORMANCE. Psychological Reports: Volume 50, Issue, pp. 593-594.

Chapter Eight
68. *http://www.brainyquote.com/quotes/authors/g/george_washington.html*
69. Virginia M Shiller (2003) Reward for Kids; charts and activities. Magination press.
    http://www.brainy-child.com/article/rewards.shtml
70. Okpaluba C. (2009) Life after school. CEFARRD publishers
71. *http://www.goodreads.com/author/quotes/1704404.Mark_Glamack*
72. Gregory Y. Titelman, *Random House Dictionary of Popular Proverbs and Sayings*, 1996, *ISBN 0-679-44554-4*, p. 159.

Chapter Nine
73. *http://www.brainyquote.com/quotes/authors/w/w_clement_stone.html*
74. *http://lifechangequotes.com/jim-rohn-quote-change/*
75. *http://en.wikipedia.org/wiki/Keeping_up_with_the_Joneses*
76. *http://www.brainyquote.com/quotes/quotes/o/orisonswet166020.html*
77. *http://www.urbandictionary.com/define.php?term=wannabe*
78. http://envisionnigeria.com/index.php?option=com_content&&view=article&id=636&Itemid=%20138
79. *http://www.goodreads.com/author/quotes/22033.Brian_Tracy*

Chapter Ten
80. *http://www.readbookonline.net/readOnLine/51917*
81. *http://www.sendwisecards.com/author/quotes-by-Abigail-Van-Buren*

Chapter Eleven
82. *http://www.brainyquote.com/quotes/quotes/j/josephaddi400057.html*
83. Franklin Delano Roosevelt. First Inaugural Address, March 4, 1933.
84. *http://www.brainyquote.com/quotes/quotes/t/tonyrobbin165100.html*
85. *http://www.goodreads.com/author/quotes/22033.Brian_Tracy*
86. *http://www.goodreads.com/author/quotes/16197.Don_Marquis*
87. *http://www.hsapress.co.uk/postcards/inspriation-.aspx*
88. *http://www.mlquotes.com/quotes/joseph-addison_57527/*

89. *http://shakespeare.mit.edu/richardii/richardii.5.5.html*
90. It's About Time!: 10 Smart Strategies to Avoid Time Traps and Invest Yourself Where it Matters, (Howard Publishing, 2008).
91. *http://strangewondrous.net/browse/author/h/hill+napoleon?start=11*
92. *https://en.wikiquote.org/wiki/Edward_Young*
93. http://www.ncbi.nlm.nih.gov/pubmed/18560126
94. http://www.brainyquote.com/quotes/quotes/r/rudyardkip391620.html
95. *http://www.brainyquote.com/quotes/quotes/d/dalecarneg130712.html*

Chapter Twelve

96. *http://www.brainyquote.com/quotes/authors/c/christian_nestell_bovee.html*
97. William Saint, Teresa A. Hartnett and Erich Strassner. Higher Education in Nigeria: A Status Report. Higher Education Policy, 2003, 16, pp. 259-281.
98. Federal Ministry of Education: Ministerial platform on key achievements in commemoration of the first anniversary of President Goodluck Ebele Jonathan's administration, a paper presented by the Hon Minister of Education Prof. Ruqayyatu Ahmed Rufai'I.
99. A report in 2010 recorded that Nigeria fuels the UK education sector to the tune of N246 billion; over 60 per cent of the 2012 education allocation.
100. *http://www.searchquotes.com/quotation/Failure_is_the_opportunity_to_begin_again_more_intelligently./274702/*
101. *http://www.jeffbaj.com/2012/04/man-who-thinks-he-can.html*
102. Outwitting the Devil: the secret to freedom and success. Pg 5

Chapter Thirteen

103. *http://womenshistory.about.com/library/etext/bl_wilcox_will.htm*
104. *http://www.brainyquote.com/quotes/quotes/d/deniswaitl146913.html*
105. *http://quod.lib.umich.edu/m/moa/ajf2285.0001.001?view=text&seq=93*
106. *http://www.brainyquote.com/quotes/quotes/t/thomasfull121924.html*
107. *http://thinkexist.com/quotes/a._lou_vickery/*
108. *http://www.brainyquote.com/quotes/quotes/v/vincelomba127517.html*
109. *http://quotationsbook.com/quote/30036/*
110. *http://thinkexist.com/quotes/paul_j._meyer/*
111. *http://www.google.com.ng/#hl=en&safe=off&tbo=d&sclient=psy-ab&q=Napoleon+Bonaparte+&oq=Napoleon+Bonaparte+&gs_l=serp.12...407445.407445.2.408808.1.1.0.0.0.0.0..0.0.les%3B..0.0...1c.2.yxycdCZ5t_k&pbx=1&bav=on.2,or.r_gc.r_pw.r_qf.&fp=81cc204960098cbe&bpcl=37189454&biw=1020&bih=521*
112. *http://www.chinatownconnection.com/confucius-quotes.htm*

ENDNOTES

113. *http://www.brian-rossi.com/branded_pdf/Conquering%20an%20Enemy%20Called%20Average.pdf*
114. *http://www.brainyquote.com/quotes/quotes/o/oscarwilde161916.html*

Chapter Fourteen
115. *http://www.dailybusinessquotes.com/category/les-brown/*
116. *http://www.selfhelpcollective.com/motivation-quotes.html#.UGlAtE3R5fE*
117. *https://www.stephencovey.com/7habits/7habits-habit2.php*
118. *http://www.motivatedforsuccess.com*
119. *http://thinkexist.com/quotes/mahatma_gandhi/*
120. *http://www.motivatingquotes.com/briantracy.htm*

Chapter Fifteen
121. *http://blog.johnspence.com/2012/06/90-quotes-change/*
122. *http://nzesylva.wordpress.com/2012/06/24/may-your-road-be-rough-2/*
123. *http://thinkexist.com/quotes/colin_powell/*
124. *http://www.searchquotes.com/quotes/author/Mark_Victor_Hansen/*
125. *http://www.stevepavlina.com/blog/2009/10/remove-a-limiting-belief-in-about-20-minutes/*
126. *http://www.tumblr.com/tagged/email?before=1324871258*
127. *http://en.wikiquote.org/wiki/Eleanor_Roosevelt*
128. *http://www.brainyquote.com/quotes/quotes/w/waltdisney130027.html*

Chapter Sixteen
129. *http://www.freshword.com/notw030606*
130. *http://www.briantracy.com/blog/business-success/an-accumulation-of-riches/*

Chapter Seventeen
131. *http://abrahamlincolnthemovie.com/i-will-study-and-prepare-myself-and-someday-my-chance-will-come-abraham-lincoln/*
132. *http://thinkexist.com/quotation/never_regard_study_as_a_duty_but_as_the_enviable/10125.html*
133. *http://en.wikiquote.org/wiki/Abigail_Adams*
134.
135. *http://en.wikiquote.org/wiki/Richard_Steele*

Chapter Eighteen
136. *http://www.angelfire.com/tx5/q_land/subject/ambition_success.html*
137. http://www.searchquotes.com/quotation/Age_may_wrinkle_the_face,_but_lack_of_enthusiasm_wrinkles_the_soul./8396/
138. *http://www.brainyquote.com/quotes/quotes/d/dalecarneg395503.html*
139. *More Than My Share of it All*, Clarence Leonard "Kelly" Johnson, *ISBN 0-87474-491-1*, was published in 1985.

Chapter Nineteen
140. *http://ezinearticles.com/?Top-35-Desire-Quotations&id=407419*
141. *http://www.goodreads.com/author/quotes/310550.William_Jennings_Bryan*
142. *http://www.brainyquote.com/quotes/authors/b/brian_tracy.html*
143. quotationsbook.com/quote/157/
144. http://www.dailyinspiringquotes.com/determination.shtm

Chapter Twenty
145. *http://www.goodreads.com/author/quotes/3510823.Walt_Disney_Company*
146. *http://www.ushistory.org/declaration/document/*
147. *http://www.brainyquote.com/quotes/authors/d/dorthea_brande.html*
148. *http://www.booknotes.org/Watch/95193-1/Jim+Hightower.aspx*
149. *http://famousquotesandauthors.com/authors/joseph_fort_newton_quotes.html*
150. *http://www.brainyquote.com/quotes/authors/h/herbert_prochnow.html*
151. *http://adamizinton.blogspot.com/2012_02_01_archive.html*
152. *http://powertochange.com/life/quotesonsuccess/*
153. *http://history.nasa.gov/reagan12886.html*
154. *http://www.desiquotes.com/quote/22192/*
155. *http://quotemyday.com/20436/you-seldom-get-what-you-go-after-unless-you-know-in-advance-what-you-want-maurice-switzer/*

Chapter Twenty-one
156. *http://www.goodquotes.com/quote/george-halas/nobody-who-ever-gave-his-best-regrette*
157. *http://thinkexist.com/quotation/i-ve_continued_to_recognize_the_power_individuals/297107.html*
158. *http://www.finestquotes.com/select_quote-category-Hard%20Work-page-0.htm*
159. *http://www.brainyquote.com/quotes/quotes/t/thomasaed131293.html*
160. *http://www.woopidoo.com/business_quotes/hard-work.htm*
161. *http://www.finestquotes.com/select_quote-category-Hard%20Work-page-0.htm*

Chapter Twenty-two

162. *http://www.wisdomwoods.com/if/personal-development.asp*
163. *http://www.goodreads.com/author/quotes/176386.Woodrow_Wilson*
164. David Iluebe (2005), immortal words of notable mortals. (powerful quotations with biographical information). Ade-olu printers and publishers. Back cover.
165. *http://www.goodreads.com/author/quotes/22033.Brian_Tracy*
166. *http://www.whitehouse.gov/the-press-office/remarks-president-a-national-address-americas-schoolchildren*

Chapter Twenty-three

167. Williamson M. *A Return To Love: Reflections on the Principles of A Course in Miracles*, Harper Collins, 1992. From Chapter 7, Section 3 (Pg. 190-191).

Lightning Source UK Ltd.
Milton Keynes UK
UKOW04f1651100216

268084UK00003B/61/P